Hog
Wild!

Discard

Hog Wild!

by JULIA BROWN RIDLE
illustrated by Leonard Shortall

A HARPER TROPHY BOOK
Harper & Row, Publishers
New York, Evanston, San Francisco, London

Acknowledgments:

A chance visit with Clint Gibler, an oldtimer from the Grangeville country, brought the idea for this book. He drove hogs to the railroad when a very young boy. Time, labor and Murrielle Wilson accomplished the rest. It was she who took me out to a ranch and threw rocks at hogs so that I could watch them run. She introduced me to such memory miners as Fred Callison, who knew about the nature of hogs; Clinton Reeves, who used to be a "dead-shot" with a lasso; Billy McGaffee, a past craftsman in the making of riatas; Bob Cone, who brought to life those long ago prairie days. Myrtle and Ole Freeburg offered wonderful encouragement. Carol Davis and her 5th and 6th grade classes acted as judges of the manuscript. To all, a deep felt, "I'm beholding."

For Heather, who said of this book: "You write such unexpectable things."

Contents

1	"Make It Good News, Uncle John"	1
2	Joss Has an Idea	9
3	An Invitation	17
4	In the Hog Corral	24
5	Joss Makes a Discovery	35
6	In the Box Canyon	46
7	Watch Out, Toppy!	56
8	Fight for Life	70
9	Tobias Makes an Offer	84
10	At the Swimming Hole	99
11	Getting Ready	116
12	On the Trail	126
13	Parting Company	144

14 The Short Cut   163
15 Needed: Water, Rest, and a Map   176
16 Wrong River Crossing   186
17 The Pay-off   202
18 A Last-ditch Resort   212
19 Rope a Wild Hog   224
20 End of a Dream   231

Chapter 1

"Make It Good News, Uncle John"

"There it comes, Toppy!"

A boy and his dog lay at the summit of a hill, overlooking a stage road far below. It was May, 1890, and frail new cheat grass glimmered on Idaho's lumpy hills.

"Just think, Toppy," Joss Melborne marvelled, "just think! Uncle John's on that stage down there! Uncle John and cousin Sterling, clean out here from New York state!"

The collie's response was a tremulous swish of his big feather of a tail.

"Uncle John's a famous doctor, Top," Joss continued. "He's going to fix up Pop's legs, so he can walk again."

1

The boy watched the stagecoach until it swung out of sight on an uphill grade. Then he sheared around, wrapped himself close to the dog's fire-red body, and rolled with him down the gentle slope.

Minutes later Joss sprang to his feet and hitched his patched pants back into place.

"Now we got to go get the wagon, Mr. Firetop," he announced with sudden gravity, "and meet the stage at the turnoff."

They hurried down the incline. Joss's gaze swept the rolling plateau in front of him.

You can't see the ranch from your bed, Pop, Joss thought. But you'll be well real soon now, and then we can walk over the ranch together, like we used to do.

They would know by tonight, after Uncle John's examination, just how long it would take Pop to get well. Just because he had been in bed for nine months didn't mean Uncle John couldn't fix him up good as ever.

Joss began to whistle. The whistle climbed to a loud and fervent pitch, drowning out and pushing away any doubts. Pop had to get well.

Later, when Joss jumped down from the weathered wagon seat to meet the slowing stagecoach, he was scrubbed and changed into clean clothes. He had even scraped a comb through his gnarl of wheat-colored hair, out of respect for the occasion.

The driver of the stage raised a hand in greeting. "They're here right enough, Joss!" he called. He bounced to the ground and walked back to open the stage door.

"Melborne Ranch, sirs," the driver announced with unusual ceremony.

A man, graying and fiftyish, stepped gingerly to the ground. He was very neat-looking in his dark suit, Joss thought. Horn-rimmed spectacles bridged his long, pleasant face.

Joss moved forward. Uncle John hadn't changed much since the picture that hung on the wall at home was taken.

"Howdy, Uncle John," he greeted, lifting his right hand. "Sure glad you're here."

"Joshua!" the doctor exclaimed. "By jove! How you've grown, lad!"

When he had shaken Joss's hand, the doctor turned to a small boy who had followed him from the coach.

"Sterling, here's your cousin, though you wouldn't know it. Takes after the Melbornes, for size, at least."

Joss grinned at his cousin. He sure don't look as old as me, he thought, not nearly twelve. Sterling looked more the size of his sister, Sara, two years younger and a whole head shorter than himself.

"Mighty good to see you at last, Sterling," Joss welcomed, still grinning.

Friendliness flickered in Sterling's eyes, then died. A part of a smile creased his lips for an instant, and was gone.

"How do you do?" Sterling said, very seriously and properly. He brought up a slim white hand to meet Joss's wide brown one.

Suffering sidewinders! Joss gasped to himself as he shook the proffered, very limp hand.

When all of Uncle John's and Sterling's trappings were aboard the wagon, Joss gave his uncle a hand onto the seat. Sterling quickly found a place beside his father.

When everyone was settled Joss swung the team around and headed for the ranch.

As they neared a sprawling log house nested in elm

and cottonwood trees, Uncle John sighed. "Pretty setting this, Joss! So restful to the soul!"

Joss squared his shoulders pridefully. Uncle John said things nice.

Joss began to slow the team. "There's Mom!" he sang out.

His mother was waving and running down the path in front of the house. Sara was close behind, her palms drumming the air excitedly.

When all the hugging and crying was over, everyone loaded up with cases and bags and trundled into the house.

Joss could recall but little of the next two hours. Mom

had fixed chicken and dumplings and rhubarb pie, and everyone had told her how good it was. Sara had mentioned checkers to Sterling, and soon the two were deep in a game.

Mom had told Uncle John about Tobias's mean sow, the one that ripped Pop's back so that he couldn't walk any more. Tobias was their nearest neighbor, a mile away. And as far as money went, he was as tight as drawn saddle leather.

Now Uncle John was up with Pop, up there with his black bag of medicines and instruments and Joss didn't know what all. What he did know was that he could hardly wait for Uncle John to come down. He could hardly stand to have to just sit here as if nothing unusual were taking place.

When Uncle John finally did descend the stairs, his face was flushed. Joss thought he looked angry.

"I didn't know you married such a pride-bloated man, Martha," Uncle John stormed, plopping himself into a chair.

Joss perched anxiously on the edge of his seat, waiting for his uncle to continue.

"Your husband needs an operation, Martha. He needs it very badly. He won't walk again without it. He has a fifty-fifty chance to walk with it. Now, I can't operate here, as you must know. It's going to be a touchy job at best. I'll need the benefit and assistance of my colleages back East. I wouldn't chance it otherwise."

"And he said no?" Joss's mother asked.

"On all counts, Martha!" Uncle John thundered.

"The money, of course."

"Of course! He won't accept a loan! He won't borrow on the ranch here! An out-and-out gift is an insult!" Uncle John sounded thoroughly vexed.

"How much money, John?" Mrs. Melborne asked.

"Oh, I'd say, including expenses back and forth, and for you to go with him, oh, right at five hundred dollars."

Joss's mother sighed deeply. "That's a lot of money, John, on a fifty-fifty chance. It's a lot more than we could possibly raise. I know how he feels—"

Joss could keep still no longer. He was standing, though hardly aware that he had risen from his chair.

"No!" he cried, facing his mother and uncle. "That's not right, Mom! Not right at all! Pop's got to get well. He's got to take the chance with Uncle John!"

"But how, Joss?" his mother asked. "Do you have a suggestion?"

"We'll have to make Pop take a loan from Uncle John, that's all. We could pay it back a little at a time."

"You know your father better than that, dear."

The doctor spoke. "There is one more thing I would like to stress. A time element is involved. Morris has had this injury for nine months. The condition of his spine has steadily grown worse. The longer he puts off the operation, the slimmer his chances become for recovery."

"How long we got, Uncle John?" Joss could hardly talk. "Before Pop don't have a good chance, I mean?"

The doctor considered. "Six months, I would say, at the very extreme."

Joss took a deep breath of air. Six months! Six months was a lot of time in which to raise five hundred dollars.

Joss excused himself and climbed the stairs to his bedroom.

He raised the window and rested his elbows on the sill.

Uncle John's news was good after all. Anyway, it could have been a lot worse. Pop had a chance, a good fifty-fifty chance.

"And you will get well, Pop," Joss vowed to the white slice of moon skimming the sky.

"I'm going to get to thinking hard. We'll get the money, all right. Don't you worry one smidgin bit."

Chapter 2

Joss Has an Idea

After breakfast the following morning, Joss went up to his father's room.

His jaws set into firm lines as he tapped on the door. He had an idea, a first-rate one, if Pop would just listen.

"Come in," Morris Melborne called.

Joss stepped into the room and closed the door. "Morning, Pop," he said. He swallowed on a lump in his throat. He wished his father didn't look so pale and thinned down. He picked up the only chair in the small room and carried it to the bedside.

"I had just been thinking about you, Joss, thinking how thankful I am that I have a son who can carry on the work."

"No, Pop, that's not right," Joss heard himself blurting out. "It isn't the ranch we got to think about first, it's you. We got to get you back East to Uncle John's hospital."

"So the doctor has been spilling everything, has he, son?"

"I got a idea on how to raise the money."

"Let's hear it."

"Well, it's hogs, Pop. I know you wasn't aiming to join the hog drive to Prairie Town this fall. I remember how we planned to let the hogs build up this year. But, nab it, Pop, we could save back the best sows and still have forty that would be ready by drive time. I counted this morning. Top rounded up and I counted. We can spare forty, right enough."

Morris Melborne was smiling. "Firetop is almost as good as a hired hand, isn't he? Which reminds me, Ropejon is with us for a while again. He stopped in early this morning and offered his services for a small sum."

Ropejon was the prairie's "floating" ranch hand. He drifted from ranch to ranch as the notion struck him. He asked no more pay than his meals, and occasionally clothes, when the ones on his back wore thin. And sometimes he would ask for a dime for spending money. One other thing Ropejon asked for now and again, and this gave him his name:

People said his only real interest in life was making

10

riatas. Whenever he needed a cowhide for a riata, he would ask for it, offering to do something especially difficult in payment. He was a half-wit, most folks said. He was just "Jon" when he first appeared on the prairie. Then, as years went by, people came to identify him with his rope making and called him "Ropejon."

Joss didn't think that Ropejon was a half-wit. He could make the slickest riatas in the state of Idaho.

Joss's father was speaking again. "There are lots of dogs," he was saying, reverting to the subject of dogs, "that don't make good hog dogs. Firetop is an exception, it seems."

"Me and Top could drive forty hogs to Prairie Town easy, Pop. Top's worth six men when it comes to herding hogs."

"I can believe that, son."

"It's just a hundred miles. Top and me could drive forty hogs a hundred miles just like eating apple pie."

"I believe you could, son. Do you see that slate and the chalk anywhere around?"

Joss found them on a stand and handed them to his father.

"You keep them, Joss. This is a problem for you. Ready?"

"Course, but I don't see—"

"You will, I think. All right. Put the figure 40 up at the top. Label it HOGS.

"Now, each hog will weigh somewhere around three hundred pounds, after the drive. Put the figure 300 above the figure 40 and multiply."

"Easy. Twelve thousand."

"Right you are. That number represents the approximate pounds of hog that we'll have to sell. Last year the going price was two and a half cents a pound. Multiply twelve thousand by two and a half."

"Easy again." Joss's chalk was flying. "Thirty thousand."

"And broken down, in dollars and cents?"

When Joss placed the decimal point, his jaw dropped. Three hundred dollars.

"Maybe the price will go up, Pop," he offered thinly.

"Two hundred dollars' worth, son?"

"No, I guess not."

Joss felt like someone had punched him in the stomach. Except for the hogs, he knew they didn't have a thing to sell. Sure, there were a few calves and sheep, and the wheat. But Pop wouldn't hear to using that money. That money was what they bought clothes with, and the smaller improvements for the ranch. Mom's egg-and-honey money bought the rest of the necessities.

It was the hogs that brought in the extra money that meant—well, that meant hope, mostly. Already from the hogs they had built the barn and bought livestock and fencing.

12

Through the hogs Joss had dreamed of his father's restored health. Only, he realized now, the money from them would not be enough. The total fell two hundred dollars short. Not even if they threw in all the best sows, which Pop wouldn't hear to for a minute, it wouldn't be enough for five hundred dollars.

"If we hadn't lost them five sows last summer," Joss mused aloud, "that was about ready to pig, we'd have enough by now. More'n enough."

"My carelessness, too," his father answered. "Should never have let them down in that thorn gulch. Top had a hard enough time bringing up the ones he did find."

"I wonder, Pop. I just wonder!" Joss's imagination was gathering steam. "I wonder if just maybe them hogs is still down there? We never did get down to the bottom of that gulch, remember? We was going to, and then you got hurt."

"No, son. There is no chance of those lost sows surviving down there last winter, even if they were still alive by that time. Too many coyotes and cougars. And, of course, the winter was too severe for domestic animals to survive in without some kind of shelter."

Joss nodded helplessly. He knew his father was right. He knew he was trying to tell him in a nice way not to be such a dreamhead and fool, not to grasp at straws.

"I better go see what Top's barking at," Joss said, and darted for the door.

"All right, son. Come up again soon. We've got some planning of work to do."

"Okay, Pop."

He got out of the house someway. He streaked out across the back yard and into the orchard. There, in high green grass, he flung himself down and let the sobs come.

At first, Joss didn't hear the gentle, worried whining in the grass beside him. He was making too much noise himself. When he did hear it, only inches from his ears, he flopped over and wrapped an arm around Firetop's neck. He drew the dog's head down to his chest and rubbed his red, wet face back and forth across the soft, warm fur.

He lay back then and let the bright edges of the collie's ruff tickle his nose. One arm was jackknifed under his head; the other one stroked the collie's side in short, quick pats.

"What are we going to do, Toppy?" the boy whispered.

"If Pop wasn't so tarnation stubborn about a loan. But he just can't help it. He just can't be beholding to people, not when it means risking the well-being of the family. He doesn't think about himself, see, Top. He just thinks about us—about Mom and Sara, and me, and you, too, and the ranch—"

Joss's words trailed off into thought. He was thinking about the night, three years ago, just after they had

14

moved here from Illinois. The snow was late going off that year, and coyotes were sneaking up at night to attack newborn lambs and pigs. That was before they had the barn and corrals built.

Pop had said, "You'll have to watch the meadow tonight, son. I've got to sit with old Boss. Something about twins. Think you can handle the meadow?"

And he had answered "Of course," and tried to act old and brave as Pop handed him the thirty-thirty.

He wasn't brave, though, that night. That was before Toppy. He had crouched under a large cottonwood that gave him full view of the moonlit meadow and shaken with fright. His eyes darted around, trying to see everything at once. His ears played tricks on him, causing him to think that a coyote, or even a cougar or bear, was stalking up on him.

Finally, when he thought he would have to scream and go tearing to the house, there came Pop.

He whistled out so that he, Joss, would know the sound wasn't that of a wild animal approaching.

Pop watched with him the rest of the night. They talked about how Boss came through with twins, both heifers, and how this would help the ranch grow. They talked also about the way you could hear things, out there in the dark, that weren't really there at all. That was Pop. He made you feel the nonsense of things without stuffing it down your throat.

15

"But this isn't nonsense, Pop," he said aloud now. His arm was still around the dog.

His eyes filled with quiet dreaming. Suppose Pop said, "Joss, you know we need that five hundred dollars. I can't raise it myself, of course. It's up to you, Joss, just like that time when you watched the meadow. Think you can handle it?"

"Course, Pop!" Joss exclaimed aloud. "Course I'll raise five hundred dollars. Don't you worry one smidgin bit!"

Joss bounced to his feet and stretched, still feeling the thrill of Pop's imagined words: "Think you can handle it, son?"

"Race you to the house, Mr. Firetop!" Joss challenged.

He was geared into a fast sprint before the collie could quit wagging his tail.

"I'll do it. Somehow, I'll do it," Joss chanted.

His fast-moving legs, swishing through the deep, damp grass, seemed to echo his vow.

Chapter 3

An Invitation

Joss was brought up short just outside the orchard by the sound of galloping hoofs. He climbed a fence post to investigate. When he saw that it was a bunch of neighboring ranch boys, probably coming to meet his cousin, Sterling, Joss leaped to the ground and raced toward the house to beat them there.

He almost bumped into his cousin, standing on the front porch, before he saw him and swerved.

"Woops!" Joss gasped. "Almost got you that time."

"Who are they, Joshua?"

"Huh? Joshua?" Joss repeated, looking startled. Then, "Oh. Well, just call me Joss. Some guys around."

"As you wish, Joshu—uh—Joss. We have always called you Joshua."

"From Mom's letters, I 'spect. She calls me that when she's riled at me. Come on down and get acquainted."

"All right," Sterling answered, his voice a whisper.

Introductions went fast through the five boys who had slid to the ground and were picketing their horses.

One of the fellows, called Hank, fished a new leather ball from a pocket and started pitching it around to the other boys.

Then, without warning, he yelped, "Catch!" and whacked the ball hard to Sterling.

Sterling's hand went out, but he missed it by a foot.

"I'm sorry," he apologized, and went to retrieve the ball.

"Listen to them manners, will ya?" Hank bawled, catching Sterling's toss with one hand. He zipped the ball to Joss.

Joss connected deftly and threw to a boy called Spud.

Joss wanted to laugh every time the ball was pitched to his cousin. Sterling missed every single time, some way or other.

Once when Sterling said, "I can't do this very well," Joss thought he would strangle himself, struggling to choke down howls of laughter.

After a while, Hank said, "We're wasting time on a guy that can't even catch," and stowed the ball back in his pocket.

18

"Let's do something you can do, Easterner, or whatever you said your name was."

"My name is Sterling Dunn," Sterling answered politely, approaching the bunched group with laggard steps.

"What do you do back home, Sterling?" Joss inquired.

"Oh," Sterling replied slowly, as if trying to think of something worthy of mention in the present company. "I'm not very good at sports. I know one thing, though, that you Western boys certainly do."

"Now just what do we certainly do?" Hank mimicked.

"Lassoing?" Sterling inquired tensely. "I have done some lassoing at home."

Joss would like to have turned a cartwheel at that. This would be even better than watching Sterling trying to catch a ball.

"You guys bring your ropes?"

"Yeah," Hank said, his eyes on Sterling. "We brought ropes. But maybe we don't want to rope. Maybe we just want to watch the Easterner rope."

Joss sobered a little, looking at Hank. Hank was two years older than the rest of the boys, a sort of leader. At times he acted the bully and got ornery as sin. But he was smiling now.

Joss relaxed. A lot of Hank was just hot and holler. I'll find a rope," he said and went into the house.

When he returned and handed Sterling a half-inch manilla-hard rope, Hank informed him:

"Your cousin told us he'd like to lasso a hog."

"Well, that's not what I said, exactly," Sterling interposed meekly, his hand running nervously over the rope. "Honestly, I don't believe I can do it. Hank asked me if I'd like to rope a hog, and I said I would try."

This time Joss's eyes narrowed as they glanced at Hank.

"What kind of a invitation you—"Joss began, then stopped.

Hank's back was against Sterling. Joss caught from his eye a dramatic wink. Joss glanced around and saw that the other boys were struggling to appear sober and innocent.

Joss looked at Sterling, then, and caught the deadserious expression on his face.

Joss frowned. "I guess it can't hurt nothing," he said. Then suddenly a grin broke across his face.

"You fellers get down to the corral," he said. "I'll round up a hog."

The boys rode their mounts down the path that led past the orchard and the barn to the corrals farther on. Spud allowed Sterling to ride with him on his barebacked mare.

Joss whistled to Firetop, and they sprinted down a shortcut through the orchard.

The orchard brought Joss's thoughts back to his visit there less than an hour ago.

He ran on, his mind only partially on the matter at

20

hand. It seemed kind of silly now, what he had said, feeling so positive that he could raise five hundred dollars. Five hundred dollars! He had never seen that much money in all of his life. Still—

He caught sight of Ropejon as he emerged from the orchard. Ropejon was sitting in the barn door, patching a harness. He remembered what his father had said that morning, that Ropejon had come to stay a spell.

Joss sidetracked over to the barn.

"Ropejon!" he called, rushing up to the thin, humpbacked man. "I got just a minute, but I want to know something."

Ropejon didn't look up. Joss didn't expect him to. Ropejon was like that.

"It's about money, Ropejon. I got to raise a pile of money in a hurry. Five hundred dollars, or maybe just two hundred. You got any idea how I can do it?"

Ropejon quit his patching. He was watching Joss out of the corners of his pale gray eyes. "Warm day," he said, his voice like the purring of a kitten.

"Ropejon—" Joss started to protest Ropejon's change of subject, then decided against it. You could never tell about Ropejon. He was probably thinking hard all the time.

"Okay, Ropejon," Joss said, turning away, just as if Ropejon had given him some hopeful answer.

Joss headed toward the hog pens. He was thinking

21

about Ropejon and what happened winter before last:

Ropejon had ridden into the ranch looking for odd jobs, and Pop had put him to work shoveling snow off the roofs of the barn, chicken shed, and house. He said he'd give Ropejon a nickel and his supper. In less than an hour Ropejon was in the kitchen, waiting for his meal and money. Pop couldn't believe that Ropejon had gotten through that quick and went out to investigate. It took Pop usually two or more hours to shovel off that much snow. But sure enough, all the roofs were slick and clean. That puzzled Pop. He returned to the kitchen and asked Ropejon how he did it so quick.

In his soft, humming voice, and looking at Pop from his eye corners, Ropejon said, "Used a riata, hooked it to the roof, walked around the building with t'other end. Came right off, Morris."

Joss chuckled now, remembering the look on his father's face. He broke into a whistle. Maybe Ropejon could help him with his problem, too.

Before entering the hog pen, Joss dipped his hand in a watering trough and then into a sack of meal leaning against the fence. He left the dog outside the pen. He found a sow whose pigs were a month old. "Come, pig," he invited, reaching down to the sow's snout with his meal-caked hand.

The sow grunted interestedly and got to her feet, dropping piglets in all directions. Joss led the sow out of the

22

pen, latched the gate, and started toward the small corral.

"Come, pig pig pig," he encouraged, running parallel with the sow and just a bit ahead, enticing her on.

The collie ran at the sow's hind hoofs, ready to nip her legs.

When they reached a straightaway to the corral, Joss stepped back and said, "Okay, Firetop, take that hog to the corral!"

The dog was a red glint in the sun as he swept about the sow, nipping and uttering sharp, imperative barks.

Joss stood a second, watching. The sow was moving, now, all right, grunting out her annoyance in loud complaints. But she was running nevertheless, galloping hard, and pointed straight for the gate.

Joss started running, too. He didn't want to miss a bit of the show.

Whatever got into Hank's head, to have Sterling rope a hog?

Everyone knew that it absolutely could not be done.

Chapter 4

In the Hog Corral

Hank closed the gate after the hog shot through and opened it again for Joss.

"Come on up," he invited, climbing to a top railing of the corral fence, where the other four boys were perched. "Dandy view up here."

"I'll stay down here with Top," Joss answered. He dropped to the ground and stroked Firetop's head as he watched the hog's gait slow from a gallop to a single-footed run, and on down to an abrupt stop, whereupon it commenced to root into the loose, moist ground.

"What ya waiting for, Sterleeng?" Hank heckled from the top railing. "Christmas?"

Joss wanted to burst out laughing at the funny picture

his cousin made out there, the sun shining on him like a spotlight, so dead-pan serious about roping a hog.

"Sing out when you're ready, Sterling!" he called. "Top'll sic up the sow for you."

Joss could see that Sterling knew something about a rope. The hondo—the small loop at the end of the rope that the lasso loop fed through—was a neat hitch. He held it right, too, the remainder of the rope leading out from the hondo, laying back on the hitch side.

Sterling was tossing his lasso out now, playing with it, getting the feel of it.

Nab it! Joss sat up attentively. Sterling was a first-rate rope swinger!

Joss studied the antics of his cousin closely. He was standing aside, now, as if the hog was coming right at him, swooping the loop down pretty and smooth and right-sized.

"That was a topnotcher, Sterling!" Joss called to his cousin.

Joss realized that in the words he had just uttered, complimenting Sterling, he had switched sides. He was on Sterling's side now. He realized, also, that the fellows on the fence knew that he had switched sides.

Joss stood up. "I said that was a topnotcher, Sterl!" he shouted, louder than ever. He turned and squinted up into the sun, directly at Hank.

25

For a few tense seconds there was no sound in the corral, except for the deep placid grunts of the sow rooting into the soil.

Then Hank erupted. "Now just get a load a that, will ya, guys?" he rasped. "Look who's bleating now. We come to see a hog roping, Melborne. Are we going to see it, or ain't we?"

"I'm ready, Joss," Sterling called.

"You'll see it, Hank," Joss retorted. "Sic 'em, Firetop!"

Firetop had the hog in a gallop before Joss could count ten. Funny, he thought, how a hog gets into action so quick. He'd never thought of it before, the way a hog can be standing still, and you'd think the laziest piece of life on earth, then all in a flash it can be moving at top speed.

The rope was twirling out at Sterling's side in a perfect and graceful circle. Firetop drove the hog in close, then swerved away. The rope came down, up and over the sow's head in a flawless hit.

Joss's eyes were sharp on Sterling, now. He saw the wrist of Sterling's lasso hand twist expertly. It jerked up on the rope at just the right moment, jerking and twisting, delivering leverage into the hold.

"Suffering sidewinders!" Joss breathed to himself, his admiration overflowing. "Where do you suppose he learned to rope like that?"

But hardly had Joss finished asking himself this question when the picture before his eyes exploded into something very different.

The sow had stopped, quick as lightning, and snapped back, and there was Sterling, hurtling head over heels into the soft dirt, his lasso trailing him, emptied and limp.

Joss howled in spite of himself, joining the convulsed mirth on the railing. He could not resist a cartwheel into the fresh green weeds that lined the edge of the enclosure.

When Sterling picked himself up, brushed himself off, and held his rope up to examine it, the laughter on the fence ignited anew, and Joss with it.

"Has it got a hole in it someplace, Sterl?" Joss managed to yell, between howls of mirth.

Joss's attention was caught by Ropejon. He had come close to the fence and was peering through.

"Come inside, Ropejon," Joss invited in a spent voice.

Ropejon didn't seem to hear. His eye corners were on Sterling.

Joss turned to see what his cousin was up to now.

The rope was in a neat coil in Sterling's hands, and now he let the loop out in a hesitant twirl.

The sow had come to a halt over by the fence, across from Joss, and was again rooting contentedly.

"How about it?" Joss called. "You ready for another try, Sterl?" He wondered if Sterling had seen why the rope didn't stay, that the hog's neck was larger that its head. The lasso just naturally slid right off.

Sterling nodded somewhat skeptically. But it was a signal to continue.

"Sic 'em, Firetop!"

Again the sow snorted into a gallop around the corral and headed in Sterling's direction, driven by the red demon at its haunches.

This time, Sterling's rope snaked out just as Firetop twisted away. It settled down fast and smooth over the

28

sow's hindquarters, the bottom of the loop dragging the ground for a split second.

Joss's mouth popped open as the rope gave a sudden lurch forward, shooting up and under the hog's hind hooves. And on it went, on to settle in a smooth ring around the sow's belly. Now Sterling was hitching it, getting a cinch on it.

Suffering sidewinders, but that was first-rate!

In the next fraction of time, the hog shuddered its hide like a dog shaking itself after a dunking. The rope slithered off onto the ground.

Sterling didn't fall this time. He just stood there, watching the sow single-foot away.

Joss shot a glance up to the five frantically wailing boys.

"I bet they can hear that clean to China," he muttered. He walked out to where his cousin was standing, coiling his rope.

"That was mighty slick roping, Sterl," Joss complimented. "Sure surprised me, too."

Sterling kept his eyes on the rope. "I shouldn't have tried it, I shouldn't have tried it," he was mumbling, almost in a whisper. "I should have known I can't do anything."

"Suffering sidewinders!" Joss was going on, not catching Sterling's words. "That was really slick. None of us around here can come close to that! Hey, you're not—"

Joss bent over to look into Sterling's face. "Nope," he said, straightening, feeling embarrassed to think he had imagined tears in his cousin's eyes. The sun was scorching out here.

"You mean, you mean," Sterling was stammering uncertainly, "you mean you couldn't have roped that hog either?" His hands were moving over the coil, smoothing it.

"Nope. Not me or any of the hootyowls over yonder, or anybody at all, Sterl. It just can't be done, that's all. We was just funning with you. Say, where'd you learn to rope like that, anyway?"

"Oh," Sterling started to answer.

"Hold on, Sterl," Joss said.

He swung to face the boys on the railing. They were beginning to simmer down.

"Hey, Hank!" Joss yelled, "I think I hear your Mom calling you!"

That got the fence still in a hurry.

"Say that again, Joss," Hank blared. He bounded to the ground and started out where Sterling and Joss were standing.

The other four were on the ground now also, following Hank, coaxing him to come with them and go home.

"No hurry about getting home," Hank flung back across his shoulder, and added significantly, "now."

Joss and Sterling faced the oncoming Hank. Hank was

30

about as much bigger than Joss as Joss was bigger than Sterling.

"Say that again, now, Joss," Hank demanded, stopping within a foot of the two boys.

"I said your Mom's calling you." Joss glared at Hank. His hands were beginning to double into fists.

"And just what's that supposed to mean?" Hank growled. His hands had been knotted since starting across the corral.

"It means," Joss snapped, "that you got what you come for. The show's over."

"You sure that's all it means, Melborne?"

"That's all I meant, yeah. If you want to make it mean more, go ahead."

"Okay, Melborne," Hank said, "We'll let it go at that, for now. But I won't be forgetting this, see?" His tone was ugly and threatening.

"Up to you," Joss said.

"I'll be keeping it in mind," Hank scowled.

"S'long, Joss," Spud said, wheeling away. "See you at the swimming hole."

Hank glared at Joss during the short farewells, then pivoted on a heel and stalked out of the corral.

"Hmmph!" Joss snorted, watching them leave. He raised a checkered sleeve and brushed at his sweaty face. "I don't 'spect I could have licked him anyway."

"I would have placed a wager on you, Joss," Sterling

31

confided, flashing a quick smile. Then, turning serious again, he added, "This is all my fault. If I could have just roped that hog."

Joss dropped to the ground. "Forget talk like that, Sterl. Hank likes to push himself around, that's all. And it's sure as sin that nobody can rope a hog. You tried best of anybody I seen. Where'd you say you learned to do that, Sterl?"

Sterling was down on the ground also. "Oh, Father had a patient from Texas about two years ago. He convalesced at the hospital for quite a while. He would walk over to our house for exercise. I asked him about his life in Texas, and that's what started my roping. We lassoed everything from the fence posts to our dog and cat. I thought lassoing was one thing, *the* one thing, I could do, till now."

Joss's chin was down, resting on his knees. "You can," he answered rather absently. "It's just that hogs can't be lassoed, that's all."

Joss's eyes, hazel and pensive, were on the spread of prairie beyond the corral. "Uncle John is going to make Pop walk again, if we can just raise five hundred dollars."

"I wish there was someway or other I could help," Sterling said.

Joss glanced at his cousin, thinking of what he had just said, thinking, too, of how Sterling had stood by him when it looked like he would have to plow into Hank. He decided he must have sized up his cousin wrong yesterday at the stagecoach. He told Sterling about the hogs and how his plan to make money through them had fizzled. "You got any ideas how to get it?"

"Oh," Sterling answered quickly, "I didn't mean I could think of something. I meant I could help you if you thought of something."

Joss frowned. There it was again, Sterl acting so kind of puny, like.

His thoughts left Sterling then, going back to his problem of raising money. His eyes, wandering aimlessly, fell on Ropejon, who had shuffled into the corral sometime before.

"Wonder what Ropejon's doing?" he mused. "He's eyeing that sow like he'd like to string 'er up for breakfast. Let's go see what he's up to."

The boys sauntered over to Ropejon. Joss introduced Ropejon to Sterling, then asked, "You got any ideas on how to raise that five hundred dollars yet, Ropejon?"

Ropejon didn't answer right away. When he did, it was to murmur, "A quarter-inch riata."

"Nab it, Ropejon!" Joss flared, then quit. It didn't do any good to heckle Ropejon. "Aren't you going to help me figure out how to raise five hundred dollars, Ropejon?" he asked in a calmer voice.

Ropejon was nodding, his laughing eyes still on Sterling. "A quarter-inch riata."

33

Joss felt like slapping Ropejon, slapping some sense and attention into him. But of course he did nothing of the sort. He just watched as Ropejon turned and shuffled out of the corral. He hadn't heard a word he had said before, either, there at the barn door, about helping with Pop.

Joss could do nothing but stand and stare. He couldn't even shout out what was in his mind: to go ahead if he wanted to, leave him alone to figure out how to raise the money.

He stood still and staring long after Ropejon had opened the gate and disappeared.

Chapter 5
Joss Makes a Discovery

"Are you dizzy, Joss?"

Joss heard Sterling's query as if it came from the other side of the corral. He took a deep breath and tried to pull himself together.

"Nope," he answered, "I don't think so. You hungry?"

"No, thank you, I don't feel hungry right now."

That brought a piece of a grin to Joss's face. It beat all how proper folks were from New York state.

"You want to see the ranch, then?"

"Oh, I really would love that, Joss," Sterling said seriously. "I have been hoping that you would ask me."

"Sure. We'll get this hog back to her pigs and then get

a couple horses. Some shrively apples in the barn, from last year, we could chew on."

"That would be just fine, all I could possibly eat."

Twenty minutes later the boys were saddled up and riding away from the barn, Firetop running alongside.

A brisk May breeze ruffled the horses' manes and Sterling's black, well-groomed hair. Joss's stubborn yellow shock whisked this way and that in the wind.

"You do all right in the saddle, too," Joss commended. "You want to race to that clump of cottonwood yonder?"

"All right. Now?"

"Now!"

Their mounts geared into ground-covering gallops that took them sailing over the hard-packed field road at a breath-catching speed.

When Joss saw that his cousin was keeping abreast and actually gaining an inch, he nudged his horse's flanks. "Sugar!" he implored. "Don't let Old Priss skunk you, for gosh sakes!"

Sugar flared her eyes at Old Priss. Soon they were neck and neck once more. They remained so until the cotton-woods loomed over them, feathery and lime green in their new spring leaves. They paced down to a stop.

Joss dug from a pocket some prunish-looking apples and handed a couple to Sterling. You're fun! he thought, eyeing his cousin.

"You have to go back with your Pop tomorrow?"

"Oh, I expect I do. That's the way we planned things. Not that I wouldn't enjoy staying."

"I can't get it out of my head, Sterl, about Pop." Joss jumped to the ground.

The boys fell into shaded grass. "So far," Joss confided, munching his apple, "so far, I can't think of one blamed way to raise that money. Just the hogs."

"Is this just good country for hogs, Joss? And good markets? We saw an abundance of hogs on our way up here yesterday."

"The thing is the wheat up here, Sterl, most of all." Joss gestured out to the rolling terrain ahead of them. "See all that land? It's good for nothing but dry-land wheat. It grows good here. Everybody out here grows lots of wheat, see, but they can't use it all. It's too rich for cattle, and we can't ship it out because of the freighting of it. It would take all the money we made from the sale of the wheat to hire wagons in here to haul it out to the railroad."

"And no railroad closer than Prairie Town," Sterling put in, "where Father and I left the train?"

"That's right, Sterl. It's close onto a hundred miles from here to Prairie Town. So the ranchers hereabouts thought up the idea of feeding what wheat they couldn't use to the hogs and driving the hogs to the railroad."

"And your problem is that you haven't enough hogs to drive to Prairie Town to sell for the amount of money you need?"

"That's it. We're trying to build up our herd. Pop won't let go of the Durocs. They're the best breed for making money. They get bigger'n longer than Poland-Chinas and Berkshires. We got about forty of the odd ones now. Course, if we hadn't lost so many last summer we'd have a lot more than forty by drive time."

"You mean you lost them by a contagious disease?"

"Nope. Coyotes, we think. Funny thing. Come on, I'll show you what I mean."

Inside of a minute Sugar and Old Priss were cantering through the cottonwoods with Firetop running behind. In minutes more they broke through into a sun-flooded view of the prairie that caused Sterling to gasp with amazement.

"I realized we climbed yesterday," he marvelled, "but I had no idea we were on top of the world up here."

"At first I called this place Hog Heaven," Joss said, gesturing at the crevasse-like ravine directly in front of them. "Them's serviceberry bushes you see all over down there, Sterl, them and thornberry. The hogs go wild eating up all the berries and wallering in the mud on down yonder where the creek runs through. We took our hogs down there last summer. It was cool, and there was lots to eat. We thought it would be a first-rate place for the sows, and feeders 'specially. Feeders need to get bone on for the drive."

"Bone?" Sterling looked puzzled.

38

"That just means they need to run around and get strong, get some muscle and grow big frames to hold up under their weight for the long drive to Prairie Town."

"I see. And it was down there that you lost some hogs?"

"Five sows ready to pig! That would amount to over forty feeders now, if we had em. It's funny. Me and Pop never did figure out, for sure, what did happen. We sent Top down to flush 'em out, and only forty-five came up. That left five sows missing. We sent Top back. He was gone for an hour or more and came back alone, his fur torn from the thorns and close thicket. Then me and Pop worked down in that canyon for a mile or so, in thornberry so thick and scratchy you couldn't see two feet in front of you."

"And you didn't find a trace of the missing sows?"

"Nope, and I didn't call it Hog Heaven after that. We figured to go back when we could spare a day, but we never did."

"I wonder," Sterling mused, "if they could still be down there, someplace."

"Pop said no, too many wild animals down there, and too cold a winter. Anyway, Top wouldn't of let any hogs stay down there that could wiggle out."

Despite his words, Joss, too, was thinking, but just suppose—

His eyes flicked to Sterling. "It wouldn't hurt nothing to get down in there and have a look around," he sug-

39

gested tentatively. "We got the rest of the day to fool around."

"I would enjoy exploring down there, if you would."

"Let's get to 'er, then!" Joss leaped down from the saddle. "Old Priss and Sug'll be okay here. We got hours before dark!"

Joss loosened the saddle girth on Sugar; Sterling did the same for Old Priss. "They won't stray far," Joss said. "Down to the creek, maybe, and back."

They started down through a less thicketed area, Joss leading, the collie close by.

"I always did want to come back," Joss said. "Been kind of hanging over me, like maybe there's a secret down there. I got no idea how far it is to the end of this brambly stuff, but it can't be much over five or six miles to that next hump yonder."

The going became rough and slow immediately. Over the ages the bushes had grown up so thick and intertwined that not even the path that Joss and his father had taken the previous summer could be determined.

"Snow's been gone from here only a week or so," Joss commented. "In another month this ground will be crackly and hot smelling, like it didn't have a breath of air."

Much more tramping and fighting back vines brought them to the edge of a clear rushing creek.

"Better have a drink, Sterl." Joss flopped down on his

40

stomach and pushed his head halfway into the stream. Sterling played copycat. Firetop tested the water with his nose and front paws and took a few measured laps.

The creek was hardly four feet across and not over three in the deepest places. Joss spied a crawdad under the water, almost hidden behind a rock. He pointed it out to his cousin.

"Hogs go for crawdads like crazy," he informed. "I'm surprised there's even one left."

Sterling gazed with interest at the bony, pink object. "It doesn't appear too appetizing to me," he remarked, "but of course I'm not a hog."

Joss snorted at that. "Lookit there," he said, turning around, gesturing to a cuplike hole close to the creek. "Them's waller-holes." The flooding water had seeped into the cup, turning it into a giant mudhole. "And there's more, look," Joss said, spotting similar places up and down the stream.

"Hogs root down into the ground to get cool," Joss explained, "then waller around to touch all of their body to the cool places. That's what makes waller-holes. You ready to go on?"

"Yes, thank you."

Joss led out. "We'll follow the creek now. Be easier going."

Sometime after the hot afternoon sun left them in cool shade, Joss stopped short in amazement. The rushing stream they had followed for at least four miles was gone. Completely gone!

"Wait, now," Joss said, and began to backtrack to the spot just over a bump in the terrain where they had last taken drinks from the creek.

Joss studied the hump and its immediate surroundings, the way it banked up the canyon on both sides, the way it was choked with nettles and blackcap vines. "The creek can't get through that block, Sterl."

"It must have gone underground, then," Sterling offered.

"Could it, do you suppose?"

"I think so, Joss. Water follows the strongest gravity pull. There has probably been loose rock formation here, and it gave way more easily than that hump."

Joss had crouched down and was chewing on a twig. "I wonder where it comes out."

"Look at Firetop, Joss."

The collie was standing where the left side of the hump joined the canyon wall, where the boys had passed in their skirting of the hump. The dog was looking expectantly toward his master, his tail wagging nervously.

"What's the matter, Top?" Joss crouched before the collie and patted his head. "What is it? Show me, Toppy."

At that, Firetop yipped excitedly and wheeled around. He raced down the canyon, his body twisting and turning as it bounded over boulders and across matted vines. A

42

hundred yards farther down, the dog came to a halt and looked back, his excitement increasing.

Joss shook his head. "He's got something down there, Sterl. He wants us to see it. We might as well go and get it over with. You can't insult Toppy. He pouts for a week."

The boys searched for an easier descent than the one Firetop took.

When they had reached within a few yards of Firetop, the collie swerved again, down canyon, bounding eagerly along, barking in sharp, quick yips.

"Now look, Top!" Joss called exasperatedly. "We haven't got the rest of the summer!"

"It is possible he found a hog carcass," Sterling suggested. "In that case it might prove valuable to examine it."

"I think you're on Top's side," Joss retorted. He was surprised that Sterling had not yet complained of weariness. They should be getting back. Still, they were this far. If it was a carcass Top was leading them to, he'd like to see it. Pop would like to know.

"Okay, Firetop," Joss said reluctantly, "we're coming."

This time, when the boys were close, the collie bounded straight up the canyon wall, heading directly west, instead of northwest, as the gorge pointed.

Joss muttered some treasured oaths and followed.

Shadows were beginning to fall, long and black. Only a

twinkle of sun met their eyes from the western canyon wall.

Firetop had moved on again, but this time only half as far as usual. Now he was perching on a sort of precipice of rock and gazing over its edge. He wasn't whining, now. He was just panting and swinging his gaze from what he saw to the boys, who were climbing up to him.

"I bet it's carcasses, Sterl," Joss gasped. "I bet they got crazed in a lightning storm and was running blind. Hogs do that in storms, 'specially loud thunder storms. I bet they just plumb went over this cliff. Looks like a deep drop, too."

The boys reared up beside Firetop and peered over the edge.

It wasn't too far down, about eight feet to the bottom. It wasn't even a jump-off, not straight up and down. It was slanted like the roof of a house.

As their eyes traveled down and out, the boys saw that they were gazing into a complete box canyon. It was a small one, not over three acres in all. It was surrounded completely by sloping walls. In some places, like directly across from them, the wall ran up as high as twenty and thirty feet.

Suddenly, Joss let out a startled whistle.

"Suffering sidewinders, Sterl!" he whispered. "Suffering sidewinders! Do you see what I see down there?"

"Oh," Sterling replied, his eyes darting around over

the box canyon, "I see bushes, and some berry vines, and —and the creek, Joss!" he cried triumphantly. "There's the creek again!"

"Yep," Joss came back, though his tone implied that Sterling had not yet hit on the choice discovery. "It's there, all right. Look again, Sterl. Don't you see?"

Sterling scanned the area again. His eyes were about to rove on when one black shadow moved!

It moved in a way that shadows don't move. Around it moved a lot more shadows.

Now it was Sterling's turn to whistle.

"Hogs!" he breathed, unbelievingly. "Live hogs!"

Chapter 6

In the Box Canyon

Joss and Sterling crumpled to the ground. They still stared down into the box canyon. Since Sterling's bewildered cry of a few moments ago, neither of the boys had breathed a word.

Joss was dizzy with the portent of what he saw. So many thoughts were churning in his head. How many were down there? He tried to search the area methodically, every square yard, but other thoughts crowded into his concentration. Now there was a chance for Pop! Now he could have the operation!

Joss's eyes came down to rest for an instant on the dog. His fingers closed on the collie's nose. "You knew some hogs was down here last summer, didn't you, Top, only you couldn't get 'em up 'cause hogs just plain don't hanker to climb."

Joss's gaze went back to the box canyon. "What shakes me, Sterl, is how them hogs could stay alive down there through the winter. Lookit over there, by them boulders. Snow still hanging in there a foot deep, where the sun don't get to it. Let's go count."

The boys slithered down the wall, smashing over small growth, and came to a dusty, noisy stop at the bottom of the box.

Joss reached down and jerked a long, white, lacy something from under his boot. "A snake skin!" he crowed, holding it up. "A rattler at that!"

"He certainly must have had lots of company, then," Sterling commented. He displayed an identical skin that he had unearthed.

"Makes good feed for hogs," Joss remarked thoughtfully. His eyes were scanning the immediate foreground. It was brushless, rocky, and dry.

"I bet this was a regular den of snakes before them hogs got here."

He tossed the skin away and stood up. "Maybe that's what brought 'em down here in the first place." He glanced up at the sky. "Still got a couple hours daylight, which means even if we started back home now we'd never make it by dark."

"I believe it would be impossible to become lost in that canyon," Sterling said. "We follow it back to the cottonwood slope."

Joss grinned. "How's your belly?"

"Complaining, but it just doesn't realize how lucky it is right now."

Joss whooped. "Let's start around this way. We got a lot to see before dark. Pop will want to know everything. We'll have Top round up and we'll count after bit."

The black sow they had spotted from the wall had also spotted them. She came at them now, in a flurry of curiosity, followed by six feeder-sized hogs.

"I bet them are her pigs from last fall," Joss wagered.

Warning growls from Firetop kept the sow and feeders from coming close to the boys. They grunted nervously, their beady black eyes staring.

"They're wild as anything," Joss murmured, "and half starved. Lookit their ribs stick out."

It did not require bright sunlight for the boys to see the horrible boniness of the hogs. The agony of slow starvation was in their wild eyes and long thin carcasses that only appeared long because they were so gaunt and wrung of fatness. In health, a Poland-China was only medium length compared to other breeds of hogs.

"Have to get some feed down here, come morning," Joss decided, "or we might not have these critters alive in a couple days."

He left the hogs on the run, crossing an open space

48

that brought him to a small rise of boulders around which had been many bushes and vines. Now, Joss noticed, there was nothing but stubs of growth. Everything edible had been chewed off.

Joss's heart was pounding hard. There just *had* to be more! These seven lived till now. Others had to be alive. He rounded the boulders and stopped.

His eyes flicked here and there, searching. All that he

saw was the creek, cascading round and through jumbles of rock. He shoved his disappointment aside and stepped close to the water to examine it. It ran bubbly and clear and empty of crawdads, as far as he could see.

Joss took this to be a good sign, proof that many hogs had fed here. He felt thankful for the creek, too. Without it, the hogs they did find would have perished from thirst.

Joss glanced up to see Sterling standing near by, staring at the ground. Joss crossed the distance between them. "What, Sterl?"

Then he saw. The whitening bones of carcasses were there, down in the recesses between the jagged rocks. They were clean and white in the graying air, scattered and broken.

"They look kinda fresh," Joss whispered. "No shine on 'em." He pointed over to his right. "That isn't a hog bone there, though, Sterl. Looks more like coyote."

But for the most part, their investigation of the ghastly bed of bones was not encouraging. Most of the remains could have been hogs.

"Why didn't whatever killed these kill those seven hogs over there?" Joss questioned.

"Maybe this rock cropping has been a kind of a lair for a cougar," Sterling suggested, "or even a bear."

"And what about them seven?" Joss asked, almost defiantly.

"My imagination quits on those," his cousin replied. He was frowning perplexedly.

Firetop was looking out across the creek. His ears were pointed and alert.

Joss watched the collie for a moment, then said, "What do you 'spose he sees now? Let's go find out."

They jumped the creek and headed toward the west wall. The collie ran out ahead and stopped. He turned back whining.

Joss was beginning to question the wisdom of his impulsive decision. He had no weapon whatsoever, not even a slingshot.

He caught up a sharp-edged stone. "Just in case," he told Sterling.

The solid rock wall toward which they headed was faced with massive briar vines. By the time the boys had reached the edges of the briar patch, both were armed with stones and advancing stealthily.

Faint noises now reached their ears.

"You hear that?" Joss whispered.

Sterling nodded. He didn't open his mouth.

Small, indistinct sounds were reaching them from somewhere back in the briar.

The air was now so dark that even at this close range their vision was fuzzy and blurred.

Suddenly Joss was grinning.

"Them's hog sounds, Sterl!" he choked. "Lots of hogs!"

"Yes!" Sterling was recognizing the sounds, too. "They are underneath all that vine, aren't they? All over, back in there. But why, I wonder?"

Joss slashed at his eyes with his sleeve and dropped to the ground. He pushed a vine back and reached a searching hand into the thorny alcove.

Finally his exploring hand brushed against a tiny fresh shoot of leaf. He plucked it off and drew it out. "Here's the answer, Sterl."

He put the leaf to his mouth and bit off a piece. "Yep, it's camas all right. Camas has got big roots that are good to eat. The Indians dry the roots and grind it up for flour. Hogs go for it like chicken on Sunday. Be no chore for hogs to root it up, excepting their hides would get scratched. I reckon they're too hungry to care about that."

Joss was on his feet now. "Let's find out how they got in there."

He broke into a run, edging the briar, curving with it as it closed in toward the wall.

Maybe even enough hogs for the drive! he kept singing to himself. Maybe enough for five hundred dollars! So they were half starved, so what? He'd get feed down to them someway, till they were strong enough to drive home, and then fatten them up good.

"Coming, Sterl?"

"Yes."

Where the briar met the face of the wall, the vines rose high, almost to the top of the overhanging cliff, twenty feet above. Due to the climb of vines, the base of the wall was comparatively free of growth, so that pockets and tunnels of empty space appeared under the mountainous briar. These natural arbors were made wider by the countless enterings and exits of animals.

Joss and Sterling hunched over and stepped gingerly into one of them, following Firetop.

Several feet inside, Joss paused and faced about, going down on his knees. His eyes squinted to see through the briar that enclosed him front and back.

As his eyes became more accustomed to this further degree of darkness, he saw that the entire mass of briar, which had appeared close-packed and in-grown from the outside, was undermined. This gave the outside an appearance of density, whereas in reality, looking at it from the inside, Joss saw that it was merely a shell. The major ground portions of the vines had been pushed and rammed together so that they rose into a low ceiling, like the twisted trunks of jungle trees.

Beside these trunks, beside them and behind them and in front of them, lay darker blotches. They were broad, thick shadows, moving now and again, as though stirred by a breeze.

Joss knew that these were his hogs, bedding down for the night.

"Top," Joss murmured, "you think you can round up them poor critters? Do it easy like, so's not to scare out what little life they got."

Firetop left them, going back into the jungle.

"Let's back up, Sterl, so Top can run the hogs past us."
The boys settled themselves at the entrance.

"This sticker patch is what brought the hogs through," Joss said. "The snow fell on top and formed kind of a igloo. They ate the snow and dried berries and camas root and lived. Still, it don't explain them bones down there."

"Oh, it still could be like I suggested before," Sterling said. "A cougar or bear could have returned and found hogs invading its home. It might have got some of the piglets that were too young and helpless to defend themselves. The sows would have taken refuge here, and the piglets that were left followed."

"Maybe," Joss condescended, "but I don't think hogs are that smart. I think the camas drew 'em in here, the camas and the berries. They liked it so they stayed."

"There's lots of room for conjecture, I guess," Sterling said.

"Yep," Joss replied, just as if he knew what "conjecture" meant. Sterl sure wasn't puny on words. He grabbed up a handful of loose rock and handed some of it to his cousin.

"We'll both count," he said, "to make sure. Let five hogs go by, then put one rock in your other hand. When we're done we add up the rocks in that hand and multiply by five."

No more was said as the hogs filed through the opening,

their grunting protests clabbering the gray evening air.

Now and again Firetop would follow a hog past the boys, on down into the open a short distance. From this, Joss knew that the dog didn't trust that particular animal.

"Five!" Joss said promptly, as the last hog squealed out.

"Five here, too."

"Twenty five! Suffering sidewinders!"

"And that's not counting those other seven," Sterling reminded.

"That would make thirty-two, Sterl!" Joss felt weak all over. "Plenty for the drive!"

There was no room in his thoughts now for minor worries, problems like getting food down here before it was too late; getting the hogs out of the box canyon. Not even the immediate chore of climbing out of here and back up to the cottonwoods in darkness caused him the least concern.

They had the hogs. Enough for five hundred dollars. That was all that really mattered.

Chapter 7

Watch Out, Toppy!

After what seemed like interminable hours of night-mare plodding, Joss recognized the clump of alders that marked the spot where they had met the creek on the way down. Both boys were slapping their heads to keep awake. Joss noticed dully that the golden disk in the purple sky was now peeking over their shoulders.

Except for what their feet could feel and tramp down, the boys were now exposed to the thorn thickets. They were so exhausted that thorns slashing their clothing and skin felt like mere scratches.

"Joshua! Sterling! Can you hear me?"

Of course we can hear you, Uncle John! Joss laughed in his mind. That was funny, Uncle John up there in the thicket someplace. We can see your lantern, too, Uncle John. It's bobbing around like a grasshopper!

Joss did not realize that he was only thinking these thoughts in his mind, that he hadn't said a word out loud.

"Joss! Is that you, dear? We can hear the brush moving a little!"

Joss was wide awake, now, but it took all the concentration he was able to collect to call out in answer.

"Mom! I can hear you! We're coming!"

Inwardly, he scolded Firetop for not leaving them long enough to dash up and tell Mom and Uncle John that they were coming. He groped back and touched Sterling's sleeve, only a yard behind him.

We made it, Sterl! his mind said.

Then they were out of the brush, climbing free.

It didn't seem any time at all till they were falling onto the wagon, with Mom and Uncle John hovering over them, Mom crying over their scratched faces, Uncle John smiling his relief.

Joss remembered to say, "We got hogs down there, Mom! Live hogs! Enough for five hundred dollars, all together!"

Then he let his head be pressed down by the dark blanket, enveloping him in warm and welcome sleep.

"You get in a tussle with a tom cat, Sterl?"

The boys sat across from each other over fat bowls of oatmeal, apricots, thick slices of toast with honey on top, and mugs of cool, rich milk. Both of their faces looked as though they had been scribbled on with red paint.

Sterling winced a small smile. "You're not exactly Apollo yourself."

Mrs. Melborne was kneading bread dough at one end of the table. "Your father left a message for you, Joss," she said now. "He didn't get much sleep last night, fretting over you two. He's sleeping in this morning."

"Where's Uncle John, Mom? And Sara?"

"Well, your uncle is helping Sara milk, though Sara insists she can handle it by herself. She told me last night, when you didn't come home, that she would take over the milking from now on, and that would leave you free to do other chores."

Guilt swept over Joss. Milking had completely left his mind. He'd have to get over being so forgetful or Pop wouldn't think he was capable of driving the hogs to Prairie Town.

"Did you tell Pop about the thirty-two hogs, Mom, before he went to sleep?"

"Not the exact amount, dear. You didn't say, earlier. But I repeated your message: Enough for five hundred dollars. He answered something like, 'Don't count your chickens before they're hatched.' "

"Yep," Joss said thoughtfully, "we got to get feed down there fast."

58

Belatedly, Joss recalled that his father had a message for him. He asked now what it was.

"It's Tobias, Joss. Word reached your father two days ago that Tobias has two sows down with diarrhea. Your father thinks that you had better take him some barley."

Joss frowned down at his empty cereal bowl. He guessed he shouldn't feel the way he did about Tobias. Maybe Tobias didn't know his sow had turned mean that day Pop went over to visit. Pop didn't seem to hold it against Tobias, about the accident. He was offering him barley for his sick hogs.

Joss sighed. And then there was the hog drive, and Tobias was always the big stick in that. He'd have to arrange with Tobias to go along with him to Prairie Town.

He rose from the table and stretched his body till he grimaced at the pull of sore muscles.

"Uncle John's not leaving today then?" The stage to Prairie Town came through just before noon, and no preparation to meet it seemed in evidence.

"He's staying over one more day, to let Sterling recuperate a little."

"Think you can straddle Old Priss, Sterl? Tobias's ranch is only a mile over yonder."

"I would enjoy going with you," Sterling answered, replacing his napkin neatly beside his plate.

Cantering along over a little-used wagon road, with

Firetop refreshed and prancing alongside, the boys discussed ways and means of hauling wheat down to the hogs. They decided the only solution would be to cut a trail through the thorn and load up the mule and lead her down. Sterling said he would start hacking trail as soon as they returned.

"You shouldn't have to wear yourself plumb out on your vacation, Sterl, like as if you aren't already. Sure be first rate if you could stay."

"Thank you, I would like to. But I wouldn't ask now. I believe Father is annoyed with me, delaying the trip another day."

"He didn't act mad. How do you know?"

"Oh, Father is so busy, you know. He'll consider this a waste of time, I'm afraid."

"Nab it, Sterl, he knows it wasn't your fault!"

"It was my fault, though. I slowed things up on the trail last night. You would have been home hours ahead if it hadn't been for me."

"You're full of rotten eggs, too. There's Tobias's place, that shack over there. He should live in his barn. It's a lot better looking."

Rail fencing, weathered white by the sun but in good repair, serpentined out over the prairie, marking Tobias's land.

The boys threaded through the narrow gate, closing it carefully. Hogs—it looked like hundreds to Joss—grazed on either side of the roadway, making red and black and white smudges in the bunch and cheat grass.

"See there, Sterl," Joss motioned at the hogs. "Tobias has mostly Durocs. He thinks, like Pop, that Durocs are best. They're the red ones."

"What are the black ones? And the white ones?"

"The black and black-and-white-spotted are Poland-Chinas. The blacks with the turned-up noses are Berkshires, and the whites are Chester Whites."

They rode slow, looking over the herd.

"We'll try the barn first," Joss said. "He sure won't be in his shanty this time of day."

They rode up to the open barn door and met Tobias coming toward them from the interior.

Joss hadn't seen Tobias since last fall. Coming on him quick like that, without any warning or remembering, his big black eyes glaring, he reminded Joss of a spider emerging from his hole. His first impulse was to swat him away.

"Brought you some barley, Tobias," Joss greeted, swinging down from the saddle.

Loud, quacking noises, as from ducks, reached them from the depths of the barn.

Joss began to unstrap the sack of barley from Sugar's back.

"How much your pa want for it?" Tobias shot at Joss.

"Not nothing, Tobias. Pop just thought it would help your sows get over the diarrhea. He didn't think you

61

raised any." Joss tried to instill a friendliness into his voice, but the words came out stilted and sharp.

"This is my cousin, Sterl, Tobias. He's out here from New York state. His pop's a famous doctor. He's going to fix up Pop's legs."

"Should have watched himself," Tobias barked, ignoring Sterling. "Can't tell when a sow will turn on you. Put the barley in here." A scanty jet of tobacco juice fired from his mouth onto the ground at his feet.

In your eye, Tobias! Joss thought. That's where I'd like to put it. Even his spit was tight.

"I want to talk to you about the drive, Tobias. I'd like to know when it's going to be. I'm joining up this year, if it's okay with you."

Joss heaved the bag over his shoulder and swung into the barn. Tobias and Sterling followed. Firetop stayed with the horses, as he was trained to do while visiting.

"I don't take no younguns by themselves," Tobias asserted. "Lose me time on the trail, lose me weight on the hogs."

Joss reminded himself not to flare out at Tobias. He set the sack down carefully on the dirt floor.

"You know I'm taking Pop's place, Tobias. I'd cause you no trouble. Firetop will be with me. Pop said he was good with the hogs on the drive last year."

"He got the hogs fidgety, that's what. He made them run. Hogs lost weight. I'm not taking hounds this trip,

62

and younguns only with their pas."

"But Tobias—" Joss paused in mid-phrase. His attention was caught by the peculiar way the geese were behaving. They weren't very far from him—about twenty-five feet—and they hadn't moved. They hadn't moved a foot in any direction since Joss first laid eyes on them minutes ago. There were two geese over there, glistening white in the semi-darkness. They were standing on a plank board, facing him, and quacking like fury. Joss advanced toward them slowly, as if magnetized—

And then he stopped. He gasped out loud.

That's why the geese didn't move. They couldn't. They were nailed to the planking by spikes that ran through their web feet. A bowl of grain and an iron spoon were near by.

It came to Joss, then, the reason for the geese being nailed. They couldn't move this way, and Tobias forced feed down them to get them fat. They brought a higher price when they were fat.

Joss spun around. He didn't look at Tobias.

"Let's get out of here, Sterl," he said.

Joss felt fuzzy-headed as he stepped from the dark barn into the dazzling sunlight. He wanted to get away from here.

His head was still roiling as he mounted Sugar and swung her around. He paid no heed to Firetop's uneasy whining.

Old Priss's eyes were flaring nervously as Sterling's left foot lifted into the stirrup. She was staring at a huge sow that had waddled into the roadway, not thirty feet distant. The sow was surrounded by a dozen piglets.

Old Priss skittered sideways as the stirrup brushed against her body. She was not a nervous horse, usually, but something about the sow upset her.

Sterling's foot caught in the stirrup. He hopped along with Old Priss, saying, "Whoa girl, whoa!"

Suddenly the sow grunted in maddened rage. In less than a second it was spurting forth in a furious gallop, heading straight for Sterling's hopping foot.

Too late, Joss saw the danger.

He watched, transfixed, unable to move or shout warning, as Sterling struggled to free his caught foot. Finally, it came free, but the jar tumbled Sterling to the ground.

Firetop, however, was not late. Like a bolt of lightning, he shot into the narrowing space between Sterling and the sow.

He struck the sow on the shoulders with all the strength and fury of his seventy-five pounds.

Still frozen, Joss saw this, and what happened next. He would see it in nightmares for months to come. His mind cried out: Watch out, Toppy! Watch out, Toppy! but his lips never made a sound.

Sounds of ferocious battle filled the barnyard. The whirl and twist and snarl of the encounter spanked up

64

an almost engulfing cloud of dust. It could not be determined, for a while, which was dog and which was sow. The sow was a purebred Duroc and as red as the dog.

Then there was the sound of crunching bone.

Right after that, Firetop rolled free and came to his feet. Or tried to. When he struggled to stand he fell and rolled again. He was curled into a ball and he rolled to get out of the way of the crushing pounces of the sow.

It was then that Joss realized that the crunching sound had been the cracking of bones on his dog.

The next happening was a blur in Joss's memory. He was out of the saddle, lifting a pitchfork above his head and running with it toward the sow.

His first blow to the sow was on the back of the head as it plunged after the dog.

The sow stopped, then swung groggily around, and received another strike directly on top of the skull. The sow collapsed to the ground.

Joss found Firetop and went down on hands and knees over the still form.

In one small corner of his mind he heard Tobias. He was screaming and cursing, swearing he would get double pay if Joss had killed his prize Duroc sow.

Tobias's rage was like a far-off wind to Joss, for he was experiencing a panic of fear.

"Toppy?" he cried softly.

A not-too-steady hand reached out to Firetop's terribly

still head. Joss could see little through the film on his eyes, but when he brought his hand back he knew that it was covered with blood.

"Don't be dead, Toppy," he sobbed quietly. He brushed his hand lightly over the dog's body. It seemed wet and sticky all over.

Then Sterling was beside him. He was feeling of Firetop, too.

"His heart's beating," he said. "It's slow, but it's beating."

Thansksgiving flooded Joss, only to be swept away by a new realization. These weak heartbeats might be Toppy's last.

"What do we do now, Sterl?" he asked quickly.

"Feel for severed veins. I'll take the front."

Several seconds passed, then Sterling said, "He's got an awfully deep neck tear. A big flap is torn loose. But the veins aren't touched here. He's torn on the back, too. His ruff gave him a lot of protection."

More seconds passed, then Joss cried sharply, "No! No! Sterl, his foot! It's just dangling!"

Sterling moved quickly to the other side of Joss. He grasped the dog's hind leg above the ugly red gash. He reached into a shirt pocket and tore out a clean white handkerchief and passed it to Joss.

"Tie it on right here below my hand," he instructed. "Tight."

Spiked, white bone protruded from the tourniquet. Joss forced himself to go on with the examination. Only superficial wounds were found on the remainder of the dog's body.

Sterling went back to the flaps of torn flesh on the collie's shoulders. He placed the flaps back in place and began tying them there with strands of the dog's own fur.

"I saw Father do this once," Sterling told Joss.

"That's it, Sterl. We'll get him to Uncle John. He'll know what to do."

Sterling didn't answer. He went on tying hair. Joss helped.

A shudder passed over Firetop's body.

"That might mean he is gaining consciousness," Sterling said. His face was chalk white, and the scratchings of the previous night stood out like the brilliant markings on a map.

Joss said, "We'd better make a chair out of our arms and carry him home."

Sterling nodded and rose to his feet.

After trying their arms in several different positions, the boys decided on one and arranged themselves on either side of the dog.

They kneeled down and formed a cradle under the collie and lifted him up. They started out across the barnyard. Joss called to the horses and they followed, plodding placidly along.

Tobias's rage had simmered down to a grief-stricken chant. He was pouring water by the bucketfuls over his prize sow.

As the boys carried their burden away, Tobias shrieked, "I'll get paid for this! I'll get paid!"

Joss could think of nothing to reply. He didn't even glance back. He was wondering what the one-mile trek home would do to Toppy.

Chapter 8

Fight for Life

"Something has happened to Toppy!" Sara screamed.

She had been watching for the boys to return and had spotted them coming down the road, the dog between them in their arms. She dashed out of the front yard and down the road. Tears were spilling down her cheeks by the time she reached them.

"He's going to be okay, sis. Don't bawl, now," Joss managed between gasps. "Go get the horses. They're behind a ways."

Sara left them though her sobs increased.

Uncle John and Mom were coming now.

Joss and Sterling kept on toward the house. They'd been working toward the clover in the front yard for almost an hour. They didn't stop now.

"He's torn up bad, Uncle John," Joss gasped. "But he's alive. Sure glad you're here yet. You'll know what to do."

The collie had shivered now and again during the journey home. Once he had lifted his head. This had proved a strong stimulant to the boys. Each time Firetop had moved, their steps had quickened.

Uncle John and Mom were walking with them back to the yard. Uncle John held the gate open as the boys passed through. They laid the collie down in shaded grass.

The dog sought to bring his body around to a customary position of rest, but failed. He flopped back in a sprawl.

The boys stepped back, making room for Uncle John, who was already getting down on hands and knees beside the dog.

Uncle John examined his mouth and eyes first, then went on in a general survey. Meanwhile, Joss told him what had happened.

Joss watched his uncle's face for signs of what he was thinking, but saw only a mask of calmness and concentration.

Finally, when the doctor took his eyes from the dog, they rested quietly on his nephew. "He means a lot to you, doesn't he, Joss?"

"He's okay, isn't he, Uncle John?" Joss asked in a tight voice. "I mean, you can fix him up, can't you?"

"He's a pretty mangled dog, Joss. I know how you feel. But sometimes we should think about how the other guy feels—Toppy, in this case. He's unconscious, now, and isn't feeling any pain. If he ever comes out of this coma, though, he'll feel lots of pain. He's got crushed ribs, son, besides these tears into his shoulder muscles and his foot. If he lives, his foot will have to come off. I won't tell you that it would probably be best to put him out of his misery. That's up to you. He's your dog, Joss."

Joss's eyes were red and spilling over. Tears were trailing new paths down his brown, scratched cheeks. He wasn't making a sound, just staring at Firetop. His mouth was twisting; his hands were knotting and unknotting at his sides. He wasn't aware that the others were waiting for him to speak.

At last, Joss said, "No. We won't. We won't put him out of his misery. If it's just pain, Toppy can stand that. I'll help him stand it. He wouldn't want me to—to put him out of his misery, Uncle John."

The doctor's eyes rested on Joss several seconds before he spoke. Then he said, "All right, son. About all I can do for him is to take that foot off and saw off the protruding bone while he's still unconscious, and try to save enough hide for a pad over the end of the leg where the stump will be. The rest will be up to you, and Toppy, of course. Only don't expect too much, Joss. Don't get your hopes up too far."

"Why not, Uncle John?" The tears had stopped flowing from Joss's eyes. His voice was calm and serious. "Just
why not?"

"Why, no reason, I guess, Joss," the doctor said, glancing sharply at his nephew. "I'll get my bag."

Joss sat at Firetop's head during the surgery. He talked
to the dog, patting his head lightly.

It was decided that the barn would be a better place
to care for a sick dog than the yard. The boys carried him
there, where Ropejon waited beside a bed of hay he had
fashioned.

After they had eased the collie onto the mounded bed,
Joss crouched down by Firetop's side and folded his hands.
He looked at Firetop and silently prayed for him to get
well. Sometimes his hands would go out in gentle strokes
along the collie's unwounded areas. Sometimes he would
lean close and whisper, telling him it was all right if he
had to sleep, to go right ahead, and don't worry about a
thing. He, Joss, would stay close, so there was nothing to
worry about at all.

The others stayed for a while and then wandered away.
Sara came back and placed a pan of water close to Joss, in
case Firetop would wake and be thirsty. Ropejon found
a piece of old saddle blanket and brought it over and
spread it out over the dog. Mrs. Melborne came with a
jar of soup and urged Joss to eat. Sterling came, sat down

with Joss, watched and waited with him in silence, then rose and went away.

The soup in the jar had turned cold when Firetop heaved convulsively, shuddered the length of his frame, and opened his eyes upon the world.

"Well, now!" Joss mumbled, half between a cry and a laugh. "What do you think, Top?" Joss kept his hands to himself, though they rubbed down the sides of his pants, as if commanded not to stray away.

He kept murmuring soft nonsense to the dog to let him know that everything was all right, letting him feel his pain and hurt square on without the added fuzz of outside interference.

The collie flicked his eyes at Joss, at his surroundings, off into space. Then his legs began to draw up under him.

He's going to stand up! Joss had stopped his mumbling. He watched tensely, now.

Firetop got halfway up, on three legs, then toppled back, growling his hurt. He lost consciousness.

Now Joss's hand reached out and stroked at the dog's head and thighs.

"You did good, Top, real topnotcher good. You rest some more, now. I'll be right beside you."

A half an hour later Joss was patting the collie when his hand happened to brush the dog's nose.

Fresh alarm seared through Joss. Firetop's nose felt like a coal of fire.

74

He whipped the blanket off from the dog's body. He grabbed the water pan and pushed it under the dog's nose. He lifted the limp head till the mouth touched the water.

"Drink, Toppy," he commanded gently, "drink some water."

Pleading and more pleading, more support of the dog's head, more slopping the water in the pan so Firetop would know that there was water there for his asking, brought its reward.

Another convulsive shudder shook the collie, and his head raised. His eyes opened dully. He lapped at the water five times. Then he brought his body around so that he could see it and appraised it with hot, sick eyes.

"It's a mess, sure enough, Top. We just got to up and face it. Three feet won't be so bad. I seen a man once with just one foot, and here you still got three, for gosh sakes. Them cuts on your shoulders are bad, but they'll heal up slick. And them ribs, I 'spect they'll just take time to mend by themselves and grow whole, like the time I smashed my thumb clearing rocks out of the meadow. And the fever, Top, well, I 'spect you just naturally got to have fever when you're so messed up, just so's you don't let it get too hot—"

Firetop's eyes were closed once more. Joss folded his arms across his doubled up knees and lowered his head upon them. He brooded on a way to keep the fever from getting too high.

Ropejon stood away from Joss about ten feet. He was holding a huge cowhide against his body, holding it like a shield.

Joss's straying eyes picked up Ropejon and what he was doing. He could tell that Ropejon was starting to make another riata.

Paying more attention now, Joss saw that Ropejon was cutting around the outside of the hide, cutting off a narrow strip, kind of like the way you'd cut the peeling off a spud, if you didn't want it to break before you got through.

When Ropejon had cut about a ten-foot strip, he nailed the free end to a barn support, at a height from the ground of four and a half feet. This was a good working height for Ropejon. The old man was pulling now at the nailed strip of rawhide, pulling with the oval in his hands, to which the strip was still connected. He pulled and cut and pulled some more, and when he had another ten feet sliced from the hide, he pulled it taut and nailed it to the hay rack.

Joss knew that because the hide was raw, this stretching would cause it to take any shape that Ropejon wished it to.

Joss sighed deeply, his eyes coming back to Firetop.

He felt the dog's nose again. It was as hot as August

sun on field stone. He stood up, picked up the piece of blanket and folded it in half, and began to fan a breeze over the dog's body. He fanned in great swooshes and watched the collie for telltale signs of returning consciousness.

He noticed that watery liquid was constantly draining from the shoulder wounds and from the minor cuts high on his thighs and down the one back, injured leg. He decided to leave the minor cuts alone. Toppy would want to lick himself when he got to feeling better, and these would be the only places he could reach. His attention returned to the big rips on the shoulder.

There were two, starting close to the neck and streaking out along the foreshoulder on the left side. Joss ceased his fanning long enough to bend closer for a good look. Each tear had its strap of free flesh—about two inches wide—that ran almost the length of the rip. He found that the tears were two handlengths, from neck to shoulder. It had been these that he and Sterling had tied in place earlier, with Firetop's own fur.

It was these wounds that would need his attention. Not only were these his worst outside wounds, but Toppy couldn't reach them with his tongue.

At least, Joss reflected as he resumed his fanning, Top was lucky in one way—his wounds were mostly on his left side. He could rest without bearing his weight on his hurts.

"Ropejon," Joss called now, "what do you 'spect we could do for these neck tears? They're plumb bad. They're into muscle, first off, and besides that, Top can't lick them himself."

Ropejon didn't so much as tender him with an interested glance.

Joss clamped his teeth and said no more.

The next several hours were marked by a conglomeration of small happenings.

Ropejon continued cutting his hide, patiently and mutely, until the space around him looked to Joss like a crazy man's clothesline.

And probably is, Joss thought bitterly to himself.

Then, quite abruptly, Ropejon ducked under his handiwork and disappeared from the barn.

Sara came in with the milk pail, cried a few minutes beside Firetop, and left. Joss's mother came, scolded him for not touching his soup, and carried it back to the house. She returned it thirty minutes later, warmed, and accompanied by two thick slices of bread and butter. Joss thanked her and set it aside.

Sterling and Uncle John came in toward dark. Sterling said nothing, but crouched beside the dog.

Uncle John had a bottle of alcohol and poured it over Firetop's shoulder wounds.

This brought the collie's head up with a start. He began barking in short, weird cries. His front paws came up under him and he pushed up on them. He danced them around in a circle, causing his hindquarters to pivot along behind, digging a deeper hole in the mounded hay.

"Toppy, Toppy, there now, dog." Joss was down on his knees, his hands out, brushing the collie's head as he spun around. "It's okay, Top."

Firetop quieted slowly. He sank to his stomach. His eyes were open now, hot and red. His mouth was open and his tongue was hanging. He was breathing in short, quick pants.

Joss lifted the water pan to the dog's mouth. The collie lapped it eagerly, until half the pan was gone. His eyes roved around the circle of people and then grazed over his hurts. Finally, they closed.

Joss turned to his uncle, his eyes wide and questioning.

"That was good for him, Joss, to move around like that. Though if it's a good sign, really, or not, I don't know. I think you know that he could still go at any time. His fever means his system is fighting. The question is, can he handle it, or will the fight prove too big? If his broken ribs haven't gouged or bruised too deeply any vital organs inside, if his brain concussion isn't too deep—it's those things, Joss, that are the big gamble."

"He'd just naturally have fever, though, wouldn't he, Uncle John, even without them real serious things?"

"Yes. The foot, those shoulder tears and crushed ribs, and the way he blacks out, indicating concussion, would insure a high fever. A blanket soaked in cool water and spread over his body might ease his discomfort a little."

"I'll prepare the blanket," Sterling said, rising.

"And I'm going to bed," the doctor said. "That stage comes in the morning, you know. I'll be pulling for you, son. For this, and for the hog drive to Prairie Town."

Joss stood up, facing his uncle.

"Thanks a heap," he said, when he could trust his voice. His handshake was hard and long.

Sterling returned carrying a pail of water and a blanket from the house.

Together, the boys pushed the blanket into the bucket, wrung it out damp dry, and spread it over the collie.

Firetop opened his eyes, looked around, appraised the procedure, then closed them once more.

"Does he seem hotter to you, Sterl?"

Sterling's hand brushed Firetop's nose. "It seems as though he is warmer to me."

"That's what I thought."

"I'll get another bucket of cold water," Sterling said.

Hours later the boys were still wringing, Sterling still going for colder water. Joss noticed, vaguely, that Rope-jon had returned and was puttering around over there by his cot. Sara and Joss's mother had come in, sat awhile, and gone back. Someone had lit a lantern and placed it close by.

Joss's murmuring to the dog hardly ceased, now, for the

fever was pulsing hot. It was so high that Joss didn't trust himself anymore to check it, thinking his imagination was playing tricks.

The shoulder rips had now swollen so that the fur that held the flesh together sunk into the fur coat, forming grooves in the distended flesh.

Firetop had lapped two pans of water, and, intermittently, lapsed into sleep and wakefulness, his eyes opening for brief, bloodshot seconds. His breathing came now in light, shallow gasps.

Joss felt, rather than saw, Ropejon standing over him, as he knelt over the collie. Ropejon was holding out a piece of dripping blanket.

"Fix up the shoulder," Ropejon purred. "Put it on right fresh."

"Huh?" Joss stood up. He had forgotten about Ropejon hours back. "What is it, Ropejon?"

"Mullen poultice, is what," Ropejon hummed. "Help the dog."

"Well—well, much oblige, Ropejon. Thanks!"

Joss spread the poultice over the shoulder cuts. It fitted nicely, with room to spare. The boys then spread a freshly soaked blanket over the top.

Ropejon shambled back to his cot in a distant corner, and soon the light that had glimmered there was snuffed out.

Time seemed to stand still for Joss now. He wrung the

81

blanket, spread it out, murmured, watched, and patted.

Sometime after a cool night breeze wafted through the open door, a change came over the dog. It was a calm, almost subtle change. One minute he was breathing quick and shallow, his tongue lolling, his eyes wandering sightlessly when he opened them at all. The next minute he was raising his head a little and opening his eyes. And though his eyes were still hot, Joss could see that he was focusing them clearly.

The dog's neck came around and his nose pointed down to where one of Joss's hands braced into the hay. His tongue swathed the hand in a hot, wet lick. Then, calmly, slowly, as if this were a natural, every-minute occurrence, his head swung on around until his tongue could reach the injured leg protruding from the wet blanket. This, too, he swathed in hot, wet saliva.

Then Joss knew. He knew that Firetop had won. At least he had won the first battle, and it was the hardest one.

"Toppy, Toppy," Joss cried, tears washing his cheeks, "good, good Toppy."

Joss glanced up at Sterling through his flooded eyes and saw a like development on the watery face of his cousin.

"Hey!" Joss croaked. "We're plumb bawl babies!"

Sterling nodded and broke into uncontrollable sobs.

As if this were a signal for Joss to join in, a duet was

formed of two bone-tired boys, who poured their relief and joy into the hay-strewn floor of the barn.

Later, when they decided they should stop this foolishness and put another freshly wet blanket over Firetop, Joss spied the bread and butter and soup that his mother had handed him ages ago.

"You hungry, Sterl?"

"Yes, I believe I am. Thank you."

They divided the bread and took turns drinking from the soup jar.

"Hey, you'd better go get to bed, Sterl. You'll never make it up by stage time. I'm mighty beholding the way you stayed right here and helped and all."

"I'm not going home, Joss. At least I am not going home right away, if you still want me to stay."

Joss came close to choking on his soup. "Suffering sidewinders! Did Uncle John say it was okay?"

"Yes. We talked about it. He said it would be all right."

"Do I want you?" Joss was chirping, punching Sterling in the ribs. "Well, what do you think, Sterl, what do you think?"

Chapter 9

Tobias Makes an Offer

The days and weeks immediately following Firetop's injury and near death were pressed on top of one another for the two cousins.

The first project they undertook—when they felt assured that the collie was on the mend—was to hack a trail down to the box canyon hogs.

When the trail was almost finished, Ropejon led Darkey, the mule, down it, laden with two one-hundred-pound sacks of wheat.

The hogs were so starved and wild for food that the boys and Ropejon found it wisest to throw wheat down in handfuls, walking along the edge of the rim. But try as they might, the boys could not entice one of the starving animals up and out of the box. Hogs just plain didn't like to climb.

Until they could devise a means of getting the hogs up to the ranch, Darkey and the boys would journey to the box canyon once a day.

Once, when Joss asked Sterling if he thought he could handle Darkey and the feeding so he, Joss, could get on with other work earlier in the day, Sterling had replied, "Oh, no, I couldn't possibly. I would do something wrong, and, well, like you say, I'd foul things up good."

"Nab it, Sterl," Joss had scolded, "that's no way to think. What do you think like that for?"

"I'm just not good at things by myself, that's all."

"I told you before, Sterl, that nobody can rope a hog, if that's what is still eating on you."

"I—I—" Sterling swallowed hard and went on. "If it hadn't been for me being so clumsy, Toppy wouldn't have gotten so crippled up."

"What do you mean?"

"I—I—well, I meant to tell you before. I thought probably you didn't notice, there at Tobias's, when I started to get into the saddle. I can't even be depended upon to get into a saddle by myself. My foot caught in the stirrup, and Old Priss danced with me. That is what attracted that sow, made her come at me."

"Oh," Joss said, frowning, then added, "It don't do no good, though, to blame yourself. Look at Pop—" He stopped talking because he could see that Sterling wasn't listening to him. Joss frowned again, an annoyed and ex-

85

asperated frown. He'd have to get to thinking on Sterling when he had the time.

Both boys had become interested in Ropejon's making of a riata. They had dropped off to sleep that early morning when Firetop had won his battle to live and woke to sunlight streaking through the hayloft. It glinted and sparked off the web of rawhide that Ropejon had strung there the previous night. Joss answered Sterling's query as to what it was, explaining how the ribbons of green hide had to be strung and stretched to take out the curve of the hide.

Later that day they had watched, fascinated, as Ropejon took out his pocket knife, sharpened it on a whetstone and then on his palm, and began to scrape the hair from the outside of the stripping.

They came close and watched as Ropejon poised his razor-sharp blade in one hand, skimming it precisely along at the base of the hair. The thumb and forefinger of the other hand followed behind the cutting one, holding the stripping steady and checking on the smoothness of the trim.

"That looks like absolutely perfect craftsmanship to me," Sterling praised. His eyes followed every movement of Ropejon's knotty hands.

They asked Ropejon that day if he would wait till they had a few minutes to spare each day, before proceeding with the riata, so that they might follow the entire process. Ropejon hadn't answered, but the boys noticed that if they could get down to the barn right after supper they would find Ropejon engrossed in another step of the construction.

They discovered that the next step, after the hair trimming, was the fleshing.

Ropejon took the stripping down for that. To one of the sturdy, upright posts of the barn Ropejon attached a vise, through which his sharp knife blade protruded, blade up. Over this firm, sharp edge, he worked the ribbon of hide, easing it back and forth over the blade until all the fatty tissue was removed.

Another time, after the fleshing was finished, they saw Ropejon examining the stripping for flaws. Then he cut off both ends, leaving about forty feet of perfect ribbon.

Next, Ropejon extracted from the depths of his trouser pocket a well-worn block of wood. It fit comfortably into the palm of his hand. It was more or less a square block, with a right angle cut out of one quarter, like this:

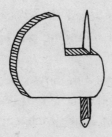

A sharp knife blade, even thinner than the one used for fleshing and trimming, was inserted up through the base of the block, in a slit so provided. On the base of the right angle a piece of sole leather was nailed.

With the knife blade firmly in place, and holding the gauge with the blade away from him, Ropejon pulled the stripping through, against the blade, cutting a strip a fraction of an inch in width. This he would repeat until the stripping was cut in six forty-foot strings.

The vegetable garden was in, the corn and potatoes planted, the beehives moved, the sheep sheared, and Firetop scampering about on his three legs when Ropejon started the braiding of the riata.

But before that, after the cutting of the strings, each string had undergone a process called edging, whereby one corner of the string had been shaved away. Then the six strands had been wound into six separate balls and immersed in barrels of tepid water, with rocks on top to hold the wiry rolls under the surface of the water. They were left there until the hide was spongy, soft, and limp.

Then Ropejon gathered the six strands, with the remainder of each ball bouncing on the floor around him, and began to braid.

It was a sight to see. The boys stood away from the flying balls of hide and watched, entranced, as Ropejon's gnarly fingers worked sure and fast, fashioning the plain strings into a beautifully intricate and thin riata.

It would have been a joyful night for Joss, witnessing such a masterpiece emerging from under the fingers of Ropejon, if he hadn't been so concerned about his box canyon hogs.

He would get the hogs up out of there someway, even if he had to dig a ramp through the rim for them to walk out on, though this solution, he knew, would require more effort and time than he could afford to give it. He'd think of something yet.

And then the drive. Pop was still tarnation stubborn, saying he couldn't drive the hogs to Prairie Town unless he joined up with Tobias.

Tobias had taken over the managing of the hog drives for years on end. Prairie folks had come to depend and count on Tobias, even though he was crotchety and short. He knew all about the weaknesses of hogs, what to do for them in a pinch, how long to drive them each day without wearing off too much precious fat. It was practically a saying on the prairie that if you went with Tobias on a hog drive, you would end up with as much as you started with. And so his undesirable ways were put up with and tolerated.

What made the shoe fit a little tighter was Tobias himself. Not only had he screamed out his hate of Joss the day of the accident, but later on he had sent word to Joss's father that his son had nearly killed his prize Duroc sow, and he wasn't about to take such a hairbrained hothead on his drive. No telling how much money he would lose on such a foolhardy gamble.

"Nab it, Pop," Joss had protested when his father had told him of Tobias's message, "he's such a mean old tightwad I wouldn't want to be in his old hog drive anyway. Heck, me and Sterl and Top could take our seventy-two hogs to Prairie Town easy. You just follow the road. And Firetop's as good as new, if that's your worry, or will be, by that time. 'Cepting for his foot, that is. He don't seem to miss it at all."

"You think about it, son," Pop had said. "I know you'll see the nonsense to it after you've considered it, thought it all out."

Well, he had thought. He had tossed it in with the hoeing and pruning and weeding and all the countless day-to-day chores, and it still sounded okay, a lot better than stitching along under spidery old Tobias's see-to.

Several days later, Joss decided that the time had come to get the hogs out. He hadn't thought of anything better than the ramp, so he told Sterling that morning that they would stay down at the box and dig all day.

They went to the barn to hunt for the pick and a shovel.

Ropejon was standing in the barn door when the boys got there. He held his newly finished riata coiled and draped over his shoulder. He stood slantwise in the door and watched from his eye corners as the boys came up. He had been waiting for them.

"You're through, Ropejon!" Joss exclaimed. "Now isn't that a beaut, Sterl! Just take a good gander at that!"

"It's by far the prettiest piece of leatherwork I ever saw, Ropejon," Sterling praised.

Ropejon lifted the shining coil from his shoulder, and almost in the same sweeping motion, shoved it into Sterling's chest, all the while laughing silently from his eyes.

"It's a present," Ropejon hummed. "I made it for you. A good lasso."

Sterling couldn't take his eyes off Ropejon. His eyes were smarting.

"Ropejon," he choked finally, "I—well, thanks, Ropejon. I never in my whole life ever expected to receive such a lovely present. I'll keep it and love it till I die, Ropejon."

Ropejon laughed softly. "A good lasso," he purred, and swung back into the barn.

"Suppose you could rope a hog with that, Sterl?" Joss's grin was wide. He had never seen his cousin so stirred up.

Sterling touched the riata lightly with his fingers.

"I wonder if I could," he murmured, almost to himself.

"You can try on our box canyon hogs in a while, if you're a mind."

"I think I will," Sterling replied, his lips parting in a quick smile.

They found the pick and shovel under a pile of feed sacks and set out for the thorn gulch. Firetop humped along close by.

Down in the box canyon, Sterling twirled on a likely and unsuspecting hog.

The riata coiled out in a graceful loop, balanced itself delicately in the air, then, in a swift dive, dropped over the head of the hog, seeming as it did so to jerk in to a tight, fast hold.

But if the rope was fast, the hog was faster. It jerked back in a startled grunt, and the riata rolled free.

Sterling bit his lip and re-coiled the riata. "I guess it

just can't be done," he said. "And here I am wasting our time."

"Nab it, Sterl, I'd keep after it, when I could spare the time. You might just up and do it, and then I'd stage a show for old Hank Ames! A real hog roping show!" Joss's eyes grew wide with this fascinating thought. It was difficult to leave it, to get his mind on the task at hand.

They chose a place for the ramp where the wall was lowest and started digging at opposite ends, Joss down in the box, Sterling on top. They would work toward each other exchanging implements as need arose, fashioning a crude ditch that would run parallel, almost, with the wall.

All went well for Joss until the hogs had finished their wheat. Then, curious, they stood close by, watching the unprecedented antics of Joss and pick and shovel. Soon they were edging closer, even though Firetop growled warningly.

"That's okay, Top," Joss admonished. "Let 'em come up. They'll do better for us on the drive if we know each other."

And so Firetop allowed more leeway, nevertheless keeping a weather eye on the ones he considered unsafe.

Soon the hogs were coming closer. Joss talked to them, sometimes nudging one gently out of the way if it got in his line of work.

When one wandered directly in front of him and began rooting into the freshly upturned soil, Joss eased his

93

shovel between its rear legs to raise it and push it out of the way.

Then something peculiar happened. The hog, helped by the support from the back, climbed the bank! It climbed a foot before toppling over from Joss's release of the shovel.

Joss stood stock still. A light was beginning to dawn.

"Hey, Sterl! Did you see that?"

"What?"

"That hog! It climbed the bank with a push from the shovel! I don't reckon we're going to need this ramp!"

Sterling climbed down and watched as Joss called a hog, got it headed up hill, shoved the shovel between its hind legs, and raised up.

The hog went scooting up the bank for two feet, then sidled off and slid back down hill.

Joss frowned and tried again.

The hog repeated its performance, climbing the bank for two or so feet, then up-ending and rolling back down.

Joss tried out several of his favorite cuss words.

"I wonder," Sterling put in. "This is just a small suggestion and probably won't work at all, but I just happened to think of my riata. Maybe if I got up above and hitched a loop over the head and foreleg, just enough hold to guide while you pushed—" Sterling broke off, becoming self-conscious. "Probably just a tomfool notion," he added lamely.

"You got it, Sterl!" Joss whooped. "First rate! The hog can't slither out because of the push from the shovel, can't topple over, neither!"

It took several tries to get the timing just right between Sterling's pull and Joss's push, but it didn't take long.

Soon the upper bank was filling with disconcerted hogs, which Firetop herded back into the brush.

Joss decided not to hurry them on the trek home, allowing them to eat and drink in leisurely intervals.

"They'll know what a nick on the rump means, though, before we get out of here," Joss commented.

They reached the hog corral late in the afternoon. After Firetop had them all in, the gate was secured, and the boys took deep breaths of relief.

Then water and feed had to be packed in and dumped in troughs. They filled one trough to the brim with whole, fresh milk, depriving the other hogs of their share for this one time.

"Celebration!" Joss told the wildly snorting newcomers.

That evening when Joss climbed the stairs for his nightly visit with his father, he was in whistling spirits.

"We got 'em now, Pop, for sure," he said, ending the day's recounting.

"And a mighty good day's work, son. And now, I hate to bring up what might seem to you at first as unpleasant news, but I feel if you will just look at it from all sides you will agree with me that it is pretty good news, after all."

"Heck, what is it, Pop?"

"Well, son, Tobias came to see me today."

"What did he want, get-well money for his Duroc?"

"No. Better news than that. He offered to take our hogs to Prairie Town."

"Suffering sidewinders! Honest, Pop?"

"Yes. With certain reservations."

"Half the hogs as payment, probably."

"He says he will take them if you and Firetop stay home."

"Stay home!" Joss exploded.

He was standing now, glaring angrily at his father.

"What do you mean, stay home, Pop? I need to be there to see that we get the money, all that is coming to us fair and square."

"I don't believe Tobias is dishonest, Joss."

"I don't see how he can help be, as money hungry as he is," Joss argued stubbornly. "And anyway, what's he want for doing this great, open-handed favor? I bet it's plenty."

"He said he would do it for three of our pure-bred Durocs."

"Suffering si— and you said you would?"

"No, of course not, not till I talked it over with you.

I do want you to consider it. I believe it to be the best solution to a difficult problem.''

"Well, I don't, Pop," Joss asserted flatly. "I know he's good with hogs and knows all about 'em, but I wouldn't trust him to hold one red cent of mine if it was just till I blinked my eyes. How can you even think on it?''

His father did not reply. Joss knew that he had said what he felt was best. Joss thought also that he detected a hurt in his father's eyes—not a physical hurt, but put there by his son's words and attitude. The look in his eyes seemed to say that he figured that the risk of the money with Tobias wasn't as great as the risk of his hog wild son.

"Goodnight, Pop. I'm sorry I acted like that."

"Goodnight, son. You needn't make up your mind right away. I told Tobias I'd let him know in a couple weeks."

"Thanks, Pop."

As he had done so many times lately before getting into bed, Joss perched on his bedroom window sill to mull over his problems.

Tonight, even with all the box canyon hogs safe in the corral and getting fat, it seemed like he was worse off than ever. He wished he could trust Tobias— Anyway, he wanted to go to Prairie Town himself. He'd been planning on it. If they didn't get five hundred dollars for the hogs, they might as well not have any. Pop wouldn't budge without the agreed-on amount.

Could a man as greedy for money as Tobias be honest?
Joss asked himself over and over.

No, Pop, Joss said to himself now. Tobias can't take
our hogs by himself. Maybe he's honest, but I can't take
a chance on that five hundred dollars. I'm going to get
to thinking on this. I sure hate to go against you, Pop, but
I'm thinking on taking them hogs to Prairie Town by
myself.

Chapter 10

At the Swimming Hole

One morning toward the end of August Joss looked at his cousin and said, "Let's go swimming, Sterl."

Sterling replied quickly, eyes bright, "I don't swim well, but I'd like to go anyway."

The swimming hole was three miles from the Melborne ranch, set into a grove of cottonwood and scrub pine.

The boys received permission and started out. Joss could hardly wait to get there and had to remind himself that this was a scorcher of a day and to go easy on the horses. No one was at the swimming hole when they arrived. Streaks of sunlight splashed across the black, shaded water.

"Last one in is a ringtailed monkey!" Joss sang out, twisting out of his shirt.

"Then I'm a ringtailed monkey already," Sterling answered, not nearly as anxious as his cousin. He tried not to appear as frightened as he felt. "I'm not good at this sort of thing, you know."

"Wheee!" Joss cried, springing up on a giant boulder. He dived into the water and managed to hit it head first, though the rest of him did a bellyflop.

Sterling waded in past his knees and began a series of wild floppings. His face wore a grim expression.

Joss swam across the pool and back several times, then helped Sterling with his strokes.

"Go at it easy, Sterl, not so all flapped up. Go limp, and just barely move your legs and arms. You can't sink!"

Joss worked at his diving and swimming under water, then they got out and toasted in the sunshine.

They were still lolling on the sunbaked grass when Hank and Spud and two others rode up.

"Well! Get a load of who's here, guys!" Hank sang out. "If it ain't little old Joss and the Easterner!"

"What you so all sweated up for, Hank?" Joss hadn't moved, except to prop his chin on his hands for a better view. He was lying on his stomach. "Cool as ice cream today."

"You don't say?" Hank's face was cranberry red. "Feel like an ice cream puff, do ya?"

"You said it."

"Well, now, ain't that just great? You hear that, guys? We got two ice cream puffs here today. Only you know something? That creek is cold enough without cream puffs getting into it. Ain't that right?"

"Sure, Hank," Spud piped. "We don't need it any colder."

"You scare the sassyfrass plumb out a me, Hank Ames," Joss retorted, smothering a yawn. "I'll be lathering out for home with my tail between my legs any minute now."

"Nice meeting you cream puffs," Hank said, walking by. "See you around again sometime."

"You will for a fact, Hank Ames."

Joss watched them meander into trees, then squinted over at his cousin.

"Hank's nature don't seem to be improved, would you say, Sterl?"

"They sound awfully scrappy," Sterling answered faintly. "Maybe we had better go home. I've had quite a sufficient swim anyway."

Joss snorted indignantly. "Not by a jugful! Sterl, you plumb unsettle me at times, like as if you don't got one lick of—well—of pride, sort of."

"I'm sorry," Sterling said quickly. "I shouldn't have said we, when I meant myself. Whatever you want to do is fine with me."

Joss sat up and frowned at his cousin. He almost said,

101

"Haven't you got a mind of your own, Sterl?" But he didn't. He didn't say it because he knew that wasn't it—not quite, anyway.

"I feel like a swim myself, Sterl," he said instead. "A long cool swim. You coming?"

"I'll go if you go, Joss."

"Let's get to 'er, then."

Joss bounced to his feet and trailed into the trees with Sterling and Firetop close behind.

Hank spotted them coming from where he sat, dripping on a boulder, across the creek.

"Sorry!" he bellowed. "No cream puffs allowed today!" Joss didn't trouble to hear him. He kept bounding from stone to stone, followed by Sterling and the dog.

Hank stood up on the boulder and poised for a dive. "Stay out, cream puff!" he shouted warningly.

Joss regained the boulder from which he had first dived off that day.

"I'd like to see you or any other lardcan stop me!" Joss yelled back.

He leaped out into the pool, spanging water in all directions.

When the splatters died down and Joss's head came out of the water, he blinked his eyes to clear them and searched around for Hank.

Hank wasn't two yards away. He was coming closer. But something was wrong.

The bully expression was gone from his suntanned face. Instead, his face was set and anxious. He was gazing past Joss to the shore, his arms barreling his body along as swiftly as he could swing one arm in front of the other.

"Not bad water at all, Hank," Joss badgered as Hank passed not a foot and a half away. "First-rate."

Hank ignored Joss. When he could touch bottom, he crawled out on one knee and his hands. The other leg was drawn up under him.

"You got another charley horse, Hank?" Spud asked, splashing out of the water.

Hank had both feet on the ground, now, and was rubbing the favored upper leg.

"Just a catch," he muttered. "Be okay in a jiffy."

Joss swam leisurely around the pool for a time, then got Sterling in, waist deep, and swam with him along the edge of the bank. They climbed out and found a big boulder to drip on. The sun was overhead, now, and shot the water with spangles of light.

"You got a hog roped yet, Sterleeng?" Hank nettled. He was separated from Sterling and Joss by a crop of boulders of various sizes. He was sitting, now, and still rubbed his thigh.

"No," Sterling answered. "I suspect I shall have to give up that ambition." As always, when disturbed, Sterling reverted to the precise language of his Eastern training.

"He hasn't given up yet, Hank," Joss interposed.

"Ropejon's made Sterl a riata. A quarter-inch. He just might rope that hog yet."

Hank snorted contemptuously. "Whistle when the show's on. I'll take bets on the hog."

"Same here," Spud put in.

"You guys and your time for lollygagging," Joss retorted, bristling. "Wish I had nothing to do but cook up some fracas to spend money on. You must have a powerful gob of time to waste. A powerful gob of money, too."

"More'n you'll have, come fall," Hank spat back. "I hear Tobias don't take no truck to fellers that let their dogs maul his hogs." He added triumphantly, "Don't reckon you'll be going on the drive to Prairie Town."

Joss was getting mad, clear down to his bones. He was so mad he couldn't speak. He was getting to his feet, glaring at Hank.

I didn't let Top maul Tobias's hog, you troublemaker, Joss's thoughts were screeching. Top don't maul a hog for the fun of it. He didn't get chopped up for the fun of it. Tobias isn't human when it comes to money. He drops any sense he's got, any kindness he's got, maybe any honesty he's got, if it seems like he'll lose a copper penny in the doing. And you're darn sure fooled about Prairie Town, Hank. I'm going, even though Pop told Tobias he could take the hogs without Top and me. Some way, I'm going.

When he could talk, Joss didn't explain all this to

Hank. He had gone beyond it, and now needed something on which to spend his soreness, the hurt that Hank had caused him. He wanted to best Hank at something, to top him in something that didn't have words connected with it at all.

"I'll take on a bet with you, Hank Ames," he said now. "Right here. You name the ticket. The price on it, too."

"Well, now, that's right interesting, Joss," Hank said, coming to his feet, also. "Let me see. This will take some study. You hear that, guys? Okay, now just don't forget it. I might need your word on it sometime."

Hank stared thoughtfully into space for several seconds, then slapped his knee and swung to Joss.

"I got it!" he yelped. "Two hogs against two, ready for the drive."

Joss nodded without a word. "That's half of it."

"Hah!" Hank yipped gleefully. His eyes were darting around from the bank to the pool to the other side of the creek and back again.

"I got the ticket, now, right enough," he said, eyes glinting. "I been hankering to have a race with rocks, under water. We'll have it right here and now!"

Joss struggled not to appear ignorant of the sport, though he couldn't imagine what it was. His cousin came to his rescue.

"I don't understand what is meant by an underwater race with rocks, Hank," Sterling said.

"Oh, now don't you, Sterleeng?" Hank mimicked, taking pains to pronounce each word very distinctly and properly. "Then let me explain. First, you must have a rock, a big, big rock, like this." Hank hoisted a rock the size of a horse's head up to his waist.

"Now, then, we carry the rock to the water, like this." Hank was still being prim and proper.

"We start here and walk with the rock to the opposite bank. The first one there with his rock wins. Do you see now, Sterleeng?"

"Don't you have to come up for air?" If Sterling was aware of the mimicry he chose to ignore it.

"Oh, yes!" Hank preened brightly. "When we can no longer walk on the creek bottom, for lack of breath, we place the rock on the bottom, come up for air, and go back down and start again. Only you must remember, Sterleeng, that the more you come up for breath, the longer it will take you."

Sterling glanced at his cousin. "You can win, Joss," he said. "I know *you* can win."

Joss was distracted for a moment by Sterling's words. It wasn't so much the words, but the emphasis on the "you" that caught his attention. Then he felt that he knew what was wrong with his cousin. Sterling had no faith. He had faith in him, Joss, and in his father, and in Pop. He had faith in everybody but himself.

Joss skipped from boulder to boulder thoughtfully.

He sized up Hank's rock and found one of similar size
and shape.

"You guys will decide who's winner," Hank said, indicating Sterling and the other three boys. "You ready?"

"Say 'go,' " Joss said. He raised the rock into his arms.
"Say 'go' for us, Spud."

Spud went through the one-for-the-money routine and
finally got around to the suspenseful "Go!"

The boys waded out in quick strides and soon were lost to sight, except for the circles in the water where they went under and bubbles where air from their slowly exhaling lungs escaped to the surface.

Joss was the first to come up for air, about a third of the way across. His face was red from pressure on empty lungs. He gulped air in loud gasps, then took one long-drawn breath and up-ended for the bottom.

His toes were sliding under when Hank shot up, purple-faced, and repeated Joss's actions. He was about six feet farther toward the opposite bank than Joss. His dive back down was strong and swift.

Joss, very red of face, came up the second time more than two-thirds of the distance across. He was back under several seconds when Hank bolted to the surface.

It was surmised by the watchers on the bank that Joss was lagging by about four feet. They were standing, now, yelling and shrieking for their favored one.

"Come on, Hank, come on!" was the loudest cry.

"Joss, you can do it!" Sterling called. "I'm positive you can do it!" He held his breath, also, when Joss went down the second time.

Neither boy came up for air again.

When they did break the water's surface with their heads, their feet were sloshing up the bank in a torrent of splash and rush and speed.

"Hank won!" Spud screeched, jumping up and down

and clapping his hands. "Hank's the winner!"

It was true that Hank's head was higher up the bank than Joss's when they laid the rocks down, but Sterling found cause to disagree.

"Hank was only higher because he is taller!" he pointed out, his voice rising to be heard above the din. "If you will notice, they put their rocks down at the same time and at the same place!"

"Liar! Liar!" one of the boys with Spud shrieked. "Hank won the race slick and clean!"

The participants were still bent over, gulping in great drafts of air, as if they would never get enough life into their lungs. When finally they turned to face their judges, Hank raised a hand.

"You're wrong, Ace," he declared. "It was a tie, fair and square."

He turned to Joss. "We got to break the tie. You want to go back?"

"Same way?"

"Same way."

"Say 'go.' "

"Say 'go,' Spud!" Hank yelled. "We're going to break this tie. We're coming back!"

This time Spud fairly screamed out the one-for-the-money, and on down to 'go.'

"Come on, Hank!" Ace called. "We're for ya! You'll do it slick!"

"You performed splendidly, Joss!" Sterling called in a high voice, striving to send his message of encouragement over that of Ace's. "I'm counting on you!"

Before "Go!" shrilled its soft echo back from the rocks, the boys were under and out of sight.

As before, Joss was the first to come up. He was more than a third across. He gulped air five times and up-tailed for the bottom.

When he lunged to the top a second time, he took a quick gauge of the distance to go and dived down for the last lap.

It was while he was under, stepping along as fast as his legs could be forced to move, that it hit him. Something wasn't going right.

Then it came to him why he knew this: when his eyes had shot over to his goal, up there on top, they also had grazed the onlookers. They had been still, very still and silent, not uttering one of the many noisy shouts and cries of encouragement or scoffing.

Joss set the rock down and shot up to the surface.

Even as he shovelled in air, he choked out, "Where's Hank?"

"He hasn't come up, Joss!" Sterling shrilled like a gust of wind, as if he had to say it all at once.

Joss flipped around and fish-tailed down toward the center of the pool. This part was deep and black. His arms fanned the water past his under-side in great swaths,

110

sweeping his body down rapidly to the creek floor.

He followed the creek bed as it lowered into the center, and as it made its sloping climb upward. His eyes searched as he progressed, his head moving in continual half-turns. He realized that his vision was curtailed, that he could see only a few feet in any direction. All that he saw was rocks on the bottom, a fish or so darting in and out, and haze, lots and lots of fuzzy, hazy water.

When he felt that his lungs would surely burst, he surfaced. He saw that he was within five feet of the opposite bank.

Gulping, he jerked around, his eyes shooting to Sterling across the creek.

They hurried on to Spud and Ace and Frank. That was all. Hank hadn't come up yet.

The boys on the opposite bank said nothing. Firetop was in the water, swimming, whining anxiously.

Joss gulped a last supply of air and went down.

At the edge of his mind, even as he pushed himself deeper and deeper, he was thinking of the boys on the bank. He couldn't blame Sterling for not jumping in to help: he could barely stay up himself. And maybe Frank, Ace's kid brother, had no business in here. But Spud and Ace—why weren't they in here, helping?

Joss moved over several feet from what he gauged to be his earlier path through the water, on the far side that Hank was assumed to be on.

As before, he found bottom and followed it to its depths.

He was about to swim on when his ever-turning eyes picked up a shaded bulk, off downstream to his right.

He angled his body sharply and swept close.

It was Hank all right. He appeared to be just standing there, resting, leaning a little into the stream's mild current.

Joss knew this not to be the case. Hank was caught.

Joss grabbed a hold on the upside-down snag as he came abreast. Its weaving branches appeared deceivingly delicate in the haze. He wrapped his knees in a vise around one of the sturdier limbs and reached down to feel around Hank's feet.

He found that one of Hank's feet was wedged into a notch in a lower limb and that the rock he had been carrying was resting on top, caught and supported there by the snag and the boulder that held the snag captive.

Joss pried the rock free and sent it sluffing away downstream, thus releasing pressure on the trapped foot. Then he loosed his hold on the snag and swept himself down to a working level with Hank's feet.

Grasping the caught foot, he forced it down and under the notch, freeing it from the hold. He caught Hank under one arm and worked for the surface.

Only now he remembered that he needed air. It seemed a mile to the top.

Once up, and with air flowing into his cramping chest, flushing the dizziness from his head, Joss got a better hold on Hank's limp body, his right arm slipping under Hank's right armpit, from the back. With his left arm and with his feet, Joss paddled for shore.

By now the boys on the bank were hysterical in their relief and in their fear. All but Sterling.

Sterling was down into the water to his knees, holding out his arms.

"You're doing great, Joss," he called, his voice calm. "This way, this way. It's shortest. I'll help you."

Sterling got Hank around the waist and together they pulled him out of the water onto the rocks.

"Place his head down, toward the creek," Sterling directed now. "His head must slant. Now we must put pressure on his lungs to press out the water. Father says it is best if you press in the rhythm of breathing."

Sterling knelt beside the body and placed his spread palms, thumbs in, on the ribs. His body leaned forward and backward with the pressure he was applying.

"I'll spell you when you say," Joss said. His own breathing was coming easier now.

Even with his mind concentrated on the task before him, Joss heard the cries around him and understood why Spud and Ace had not come to his aid. It made him feel very meek, somehow, to hear their begged forgiveness. Spud could not swim under water at all, he said over and over; he just couldn't manage to stay down no matter how hard he tried. Ace could swim under, but could not bring himself to open his eyes; he could see nothing while swimming under the surface.

Sterling and Joss had interchanged two times when Hank's body jerked, and he took in a strangled gasp of air.

In the next minutes, as Joss and Sterling continued their ministrations, Hank's body writhed to and fro, his mouth sucking in gasps of air. And then his breathing came evenly.

He opened his eyes. He said nothing for a long time, just rolled his eyes weakly, closing them now and then.

The first words he choked out were "I'm beholding."

More time passed.

Rays from a setting sun shredded through the trees and glinted across the water.

Joss and Sterling had moved Hank back away from the water's edge, back to a spot of sunshine and warmth. They had covered him with their shirts.

Then Hank was sitting up. He braced his head into his palms.

"Charley horse," Hank said in a tired voice. "Charley horse, Joss, in my free leg. Couldn't move. Couldn't work myself loose."

Next, Hank was up on his feet, taking slow, feeble steps.

"Seems good," he said. "Never thought I'd walk on dry land again."

When Hank felt strong enough to get into the saddle, Ace got the horse and Spud held the stirrup while Joss and Sterling helped to brace Hank's wobbly frame.

When he was in the saddle and grasping the reins, the others got their horses and mounted.

"I'll see you home, Hank," Spud said.

"I'll not be forgetting this, Joss, Sterl," Hank said, staring at his horse's mane. He didn't trust himself to turn his head, lest he topple off.

"I'll not be forgetting."

"Take it easy," Joss advised, and watched as Hank, even in his weakness, led the way out to the road.

But Joss knew, and all the others knew, that Hank wouldn't be the same for quite a while.

Chapter 11

Getting Ready

Tobias set October first as the starting date for the drive. He paid a visit to Joss's father to tell him this, and also to compromise about Joss going along. Joss could go, Tobias told the sick man on the bed, but that snake-in-the-grass collie would have to stay home. That was the final word.

Joss didn't take to Tobias's offer at first. Keeping seventy-two hogs in line without Firetop, for over a week and in strange territory, seemed to him like a nightmare struggle. Besides, Joss asked himself, what made old skin-flint change his mind, anyway?

When Joss asked why Tobias had changed his mind, his father answered, "I can't say, exactly. But I have an idea it was from pressure. Pressure from the fathers of your pals, Hank and Spud. They visited Tobias, it seems, and reasoned with him that a boy who could save another boy from drowning, in such a way as you did, just wasn't as bad as Tobias seemed to think."

That was the reason, then, but still, Joss didn't like the idea. Then two things happened to change his mind.

The first was Firetop himself.

He looked healthy and healed up, now, and he worked hard on his three legs, taking the hogs out to the stubble-fields. The hogs were taken there to fatten on the fallen wheat and stalks. Firetop watched them closely to see that none went astray and brought them in at night.

The third evening that the collie came in with the hogs, Joss noticed that he limped on his one hind leg.

Joss lifted the foot to examine it. He found that the paw was thin, awfully thin and worn, and that blood drained from it in places, like it was seeping through a sponge.

"Top!" Joss cried, "I been working you too hard, not remembering you got just one foot to take the brunt of all that stubble."

Joss and Sterling took the hogs out the next day. Joss locked Firetop in the barn.

When they came in that evening, weary and hot, Fire-top bounded to meet them, and with hardly a wag of his tail and shake of his head, darted around to take over the chore of pointing the hogs into the corral.

"What's he got on that foot, Sterl?" Joss asked, perplexed.

"Looks like a padding of some kind."

When the collie returned, wheeling up to Joss, the boys examined his foot and discovered that he was wearing a shoe, comprised of a round of soft leather in which his foot was set, the edges gathered up around the leg and fastened.

"Ropejon!" Joss cried, grinning and chuckling all at once. "Ropejon fixed you up again, didn't he, Top?"

The boys found Ropejon enlarging Mrs. Melborne's potato cellar.

"How'd you think of that, Ropejon?" Joss questioned, after he had thanked the man.

Ropejon eyed Joss from his birdlike eyes and went on with his work.

"Well, much oblige, Ropejon. Now Top can work in the stubblefields good as ever."

And though Firetop did perform in splendid style after that, Joss watched him more closely and decided that the collie wasn't as good as ever. Not really. Not only was the foot taking on the added strain of the lost one, but the muscles on that side of him, all of them, were taking on double duty. He was sure, now, that Firetop looked thinner and less healthy after a week in the stubblefields. It wouldn't matter, most of the time, about Toppy's weak side, because he didn't work so hard all the time.

118

He just worked hard, now, when the hogs had to be taken out to fatten before the drive.

And on the drive—Firetop would have to work hard on the drive. When he thought of this, Joss was thankful for Tobias's conditions.

The second thing that happened to change Joss's mind about not liking Tobias's offer was Tobias.

Hank had ridden over one day to tell him that Tobias's sow, the one that attacked Firetop, was getting so mean and unruly that Tobias was putting her in with the drive hogs, to sell her for meat.

That news cinched Joss's mind about the collie. Firetop would definitely stay home this trip.

At least, Joss thought, trying to find a bright side in the matter, Tobias wasn't asking for three of Pop's purebred Durocs anymore. He was going to take him along just like any other rancher and his herd of hogs.

School would take up after the boys returned. Sterling had obtained permission from his father to stay until after the drive.

The last of the wheat and the hay was in, now. The weather held balmy and dry. An occasional thunder and lightning storm split the prairie sky into bright and flaming pieces, like an exploded jigsaw puzzle.

The week before the drive Joss had so much to accomplish he wondered if he and Sterling and Ropejon, with Mom and Sara pitching in, would get it all finished.

119

The potatoes had to be dug and loaded on the wagon and hauled to the cellar. The onions, too. The cabbages had to be pulled and buried; the carrots also. The corn would need gathering, shucking, and tossing in the corn cribs. Mom and Sara would tend to the dry beans, squashes and pumpkins later.

Then there were the box canyon hogs to mark, a job Joss had been putting off but was now forced to attend to.

Each rancher taking hogs on the drive would clip the right ear of each of his hogs with his own, personal, identifying mark. This way there would be no dispute, at the drive's end, over what hogs belonged to whom. The mark Morris Melborne had taken was the underbit. This was a small cut into the right ear, close down to the head, like this:

Other marks, used by other ranches, were:

overbit   the crop   overslope   halfcrop   underslope   swallowfork

Variations of these were used if more marks were needed.

120

Joss and Sterling marked hogs for two evenings. Joss's father had, several summers ago, devised a chute for this special chore.

Firetop chased the hogs in, one at a time. All that a hog saw, when it rumbled into the cage, was Joss's meal-caked hand, just outside, at the far end. Without exception, each hog would stick its snout through the bars— fitted just for its head—to reach the meal. While the hog was reaching, Joss would cut in with his sharp knife, clipping the right ear. When this was done, the frame was lifted and the hog escaped. Joss sighed gratefully when the job was completed.

The night before the drive the boys tramped wearily into Morris Melborne's bedroom for their daily visit and last-minute instructions.

It had been a day with hardly a spare breath between the many chores and preparations. But it had been an exciting day, too, and not far under the crust of heavy tiredness dwelt the sparkle of thrill: tomorrow was the long-awaited day!

"We got the wagon loaded, Pop!" Joss announced. He dropped to the floor beside his father's bed.

"Wheat and corn's packed tight, and grub, and cooking things for Sterl and me. All we need to throw in come morning is the blankets."

It seemed to Joss that his father had grown thinner and more pale through these hot summer months, but

121

he told himself quickly that he was just imagining again.

"It won't be long now, Pop. Just think, in less than a month you'll be fixing to get your operation!"

Morris Melborne sighed lightly. He opened his sickly lips to speak, and then closed them again.

"I know what you was going to say, Pop. But the prices for hogs aren't going to drop this year. Hank and some others was saying that the price had hiked a half-cent! And if it has, Pop, why me and Sterl have got something figured out. Not just Mom's going with you, but Sara and me, too! Sterl said his tutor could fix us up with lessons so's not to get behind in school. We could all see what it's like back there—and—and be with you when you walk, Pop!"

"And the ranch, son?" Morris Melborne was smiling a little.

"We got that figured out, too. We could tell Ropejon what the score is. He could hold down the ranch for a few months. Top would be here, too."

Joss's father turned his head to gaze thoughtfully out of the window.

The harvest moon, as new and bright as a polished pumpkin, was tipping into the gray bowl of the sky.

"Dream castles aren't a loss, really," Joss's father said, his eyes still gazing into the heavens. "They're fun, while you're blowing them up. And who knows, they might

122

turn out to be more than dream castles, and then look where you'd be."

The sick man turned back to the boys. "It's a fine dream, Joss. Care if I join you?"

"You mean, you mean—" Joss stammered. "You mean I'm not so—well—so allfired hog wild after all, Pop?" Joss had never, in his wildest thoughts, hoped that his father would understand about his dreaming. When he did spill them out, his desires and dreams, it was because he just had to tell them.

"No," Joss's father denied, "I meant you are hog wild, as you call it, jumping to the moon in your mind, then trying to get there with your feet. Sometimes a man has to be hog wild, son."

He held out a frail, white hand. "Good luck, boys. Get a good night's rest, now. I'll be ready for that journey East when you get back."

Sterling was the first to shake the proffered hand. "Joss will do splendidly, Uncle Morris," he vouched. "I know we'll come back with five hundred dollars."

"Pop," Joss ground out. He wished the lump would get out of his throat. "Thanks, Pop. You be eating real first-rate now, to get in shape for that trip."

"I'll do that, son. One more thing. I think you'd better take the thirty-thirty. Probably won't need it at all, but I'll feel better if you have it along."

123

"Okay, Pop. We'll put it in the wagon. Goodnight."

The next morning the boys were up an hour before daylight.

With hearty breakfasts straining their belts the boys told Mrs. Melborne goodbye. Sara, also, crept down in her nightgown to bid farewells.

Sugar and Old Priss were hitched to the wagon.

Sterling climbed to the driver's seat. The boys would spell each other driving and herding. Sterling resembled any other rancher's son this morning, his hat brim pulled down to house his hair that had not been cut since his arrival. His new riata swung from his waist in glistening coils.

Joss directed Firetop to bring the hogs to an open area beyond the house. Then he walked with the collie back to the barn. He talked to the dog as they went along, explaining to him why he couldn't go along this trip.

In the barn Joss slipped a rope loop over the collie's head and cinched it down snug. He fastened the other end to a barn support. He admonished Ropejon not to let the dog off the loop for three days.

"He'd follow us, Ropejon, and then I don't know what I'd do."

"So long," Ropejon murmured.

Joss began to move the herd. With the aid of a sling-shot and a pocket of rocks, a stick, and sheer determined

124

shoving, he got the hogs headed out to the main road where he would meet Tobias.

He worked frantically, yelling and pushing and flipping small stones, running from one side of the herd to the other.

But even so, his ears picked up a sound reaching him from over the rumble and grunts of seventy-two hogs on the move.

The sound was Firetop. He was asking in high, anguished wails why he had to be left behind.

Chapter 12

On the Trail

"Get back there, you ringtailed varmit!"

Joss let go a rock from his sling that connected deftly with the hindquarters of a straying hog. The animal, squeaking sharply, leaped back into the moving herd.

Joss dug into a pocket for more ammunition, his eyes seeking new targets. So far, so good. They were almost to the main road.

Dust, sworling up into the sunrise, told Joss that Tobias must be on time.

"Hyah there, Joss!"

Joss could barely make out Tobias's giant feed wagon through the orange-tinted blur ahead.

"Tobias!" Joss yelled. "Right here, Tobias!"

"I know where you are!" Tobias's voice clanged. "Hold

your hogs up till I get by. Fall in at the tail, hear?"

"Yes, sir!" Joss shouted, and bolted into a run.

He skirted the right flank of his herd and gestured to Sterling to turn left and halt.

Sterling copied Joss's antics with slingshot and rocks, chasing a hog that defied guidance.

Sweat was streaming down the boys' red and already mudcaked cheeks when the last of Tobias's herd rumbled by, Hank bringing up the rear.

No one had time this morning to fling out friendly insults or hardly to wave in passing. Hank's father was away on business, and Tobias had taken over his hogs. Hank was on the drive as one of Tobias's hired hands; he was busy now, too, chasing wandering hogs back into the flock, keeping them moving in one direction.

Joss and Sterling endured the clouds of dust at the tail of the herd for some time, then Joss called a halt.

"We'll hold back a hundred yards," he choked, dashing up to his cousin. "Leastways, we'll just have our own muck then."

It proved not to be as simple as that. The Melborne hogs were feeling neighborly and were leaping and shooting ahead, seeming not to mind the haze they were in.

Sterling sprang from the wagon and headed round the opposite side from which Joss had disappeared, and soon he, too, was out of sight.

Joss realized almost instantly that what he had intended

to do, separate his hogs from the rear of Tobias's herd, would be impossible. He had thought of it too late. Who could separate seventy-two pinbrained, single-action, blind and sociable hogs from three hundred of the same? Nobody on earth could do that inside of a day, except Firetop, and he was safe at home.

Joss turned back. He was alone in great clouds of settling dust. He edged around out of the maze and went in search of Sterling. He found him a hundred feet farther on. He was standing still, out of the main track of dust. He was looking down.

Joss saw in a glance that Sterling was staring down at a hog lying still at his feet.

Fear clutched at Joss. Had they lost a hog already, and not an hour from home?

"What, Sterl?" he gasped.

Then Joss whooped. "Suffering sidewinders! You did it, Sterl? You lassoed a hog dead still?"

Sterling's smile cut a wide crack in his mudcaked face. "It's the riata, Joss. The riata makes all the difference. It holds in the short hair. I think I've finally got the knack of it."

Joss went down on his knees. "You bulldogged it, too!" The riata ran snugly around the hog's neck and inside one foreleg, then out and around the legs, binding them tight and immovable.

Old Priss, whinnying protestingly close by, brought them from distraction.

Joss rose and gazed in the direction of the dust clouds, receding in the distance. The still animal at their feet was the only hog in sight.

"We're in for it, now," Joss mumbled to himself.

Sterling loosened the riata. "I shouldn't have tried it. Not now. This is my fault."

"I did the fool trick, Sterl, heading the hogs in so close behind Tobias. Can't nobody get 'em all sorted out now till stopping time. Looks to me like it would be simpler to drive in one big herd anyway, everybody helping everybody. I'll get up to the front and suggest that to him, before he has a chance to plow right down my middle."

"Ill bring the wagon," Sterling said. He slapped the freed hog on the rump. It sprang up snorting and was bounding toward the fading dirt clouds before Joss had taken two steps.

Joss broke into a run, skirting the herd. He passed Spud and two herders and told them nothing was wrong; he was just going up to talk to Tobias. He didn't see Hank and decided he must be on the other side of the herd.

He wished the slight breeze that was blowing would change course. He should be used to the smell of hogs by now, he reasoned, wrinkling his nose. But he'd never been around such a big, squashed-up mess of them before, either.

Tobias's wagon was out ahead by several yards. He was driving down the center of the road, moving at the steady pace of a leisurely walk.

As Joss pointed in toward the wagon he watched for the mean sow. They all looked the same from the front, their red-brown heads rocking easy as they tumbled along, rolling from the momentum of the push from behind.

"Tobias!" Joss called, catching up and walking alongside the huge feed wagon drawn by four horses.

Without any kind of introduction, Joss stated his business. "I was wondering how you'd take to mixing the herds, Tobias? That's what happened back there. They ran together. We can't separate 'em, now. Looks to me like it'd be better anyway, all of us herding one big bunch. What do you figure, Tobias?"

Joss looked squarely at Tobias and was glad that he had spoken all at once. Tobias was turning a dull red under his several layers of prairie sand. His pinched face seemed to puff up, like bread dough.

"I'll not put up with any truck from upstarts!" Tobias snapped, his voice shrill and dry.

"If it wasn't for telling your pa I'd take you along I'd leave you right now. I'll give you one more chance to act

130

like a hand. When we stop in the afternoon to rest and feed, you separate your hogs and get to the rear. Keep your place till the hogs are in the pens at Prairie Town. When we take on more bunches, along toward sundown, you fall back, let them get between. I want you at the rear, as far away as possible."

Joss opened his mouth to ask why, but clamped it closed. He had reminded himself all the way up here to be civil, to be civil for Pop's sake. He swung around, now, without a word, and skirted back along the herd. He took a station halfway between Spud and the next driver and groped along, running or walking his beat as the hours dragged by.

Sometimes he fanned out from the herd to check on Sterling's progress with the feed wagon. He was always there, a hand ready to wave, driving the slow, monotonous, hot and dusty miles in apparent good spirits.

Early in the afternoon Tobias stopped; by that time Joss had figured out a plan to separate his hogs. He left the herd and ran back to where Sterling had halted the feed wagon. He told Sterling to get the wagon turned around and drive back a hundred yards.

Sterling did as he was bidden, following Joss's lead. Joss found a likely spot, close to the slow running stream, where the bank was low. They unhitched the wagon and dug out some oats for the horses.

"Now then, Sterl, we got to get our hogs back here.

Tobias said so. We got to get 'em and keep 'em right smack back here all the way. We'll give 'em a lesson on where they're supposed to be right now. Get out a sack of them shorts and midlins. Spill half of it around the wagon in scraggly streams, then come on up and give me a hand."

Joss got a bucket, filled it with wheat mash, and turned back to the herd.

He found a pocket of his hogs in a narrow gully at the edge of the main flock. Most of his hogs would be easy to find, as the majority were of Poland-China stock. His half-breed Durocs would be the most difficult since their coloring was almost identical to Tobias's purebred Durocs'. And then Tobias, too, had some off-breeds and other breeds in the drive.

He neared his bunch of hogs, his hand outstretched, filled with wheat mash.

"Come, pig," he invited in low tones, passing his hand under the snouts of several, then easing away, retreating slowly so that he would not alarm nor attract other hogs feeding close by. Eight underbit marked hogs surged in Joss's wake, grunting in anticipation of a feed of wheat. In minutes they were back at the wagon, the eight hogs busily rooting up the feed spilled onto the grassy embankment.

"Sixty-four to go, Sterl," Joss called as they both headed back toward the herd.

Sterling found five underbits together on the bank of the stream and lured them back to the wagon as Joss had done. Joss followed with five more.

"Fifty-four," Joss sighed as they swung back. "They all aren't going to be in bunches."

Hank signaled to the returning boys. He had spotted six scattered near him. Joss and Sterling got them into one bunch, found two more to put with them, and Sterling took them back.

When one of Tobias's hogs smelled feed and snorted along, a sharp clip from the side of a palm or knee was sufficient to send it grunting away. Tobias stood off to the side, by his wagon, watching the boys' methods, waiting for them to get their hogs out before he began to feed his own.

Hank muttered in Joss's ear, "Old skinflint can't think of feeding yet. Might lose a handful of corn to a underbit."

Once Tobias called stridently, "I won't wait all afternoon! I know faster ways than this to get rid of poachers!"

Joss glanced up, his face red and splotched with mud and sweat, and said nothing.

Another time, Tobias clanged, "Another kick like that to my hogs and you'll quit. I'll put my mark on what's left of yours. They'll be mine!"

Joss had nothing to say in reply. "Cut 'em out with

133

your back to him," Joss instructed Sterling when they were close enough to talk.

Forty minutes later all the underbits but four were milling around the Melborne feed wagon or drinking from the creek.

The boys exchanged worried glances as they tramped back for the four. The other herders had helped them to spot and separate, when they could do so without engaging Tobias's wrath. The herd had spread out over three acres of sloping ground and the herders were kept busy in their own right, keeping the hungry, hot, and tired animals in one spread-out group. But they were also in positions to spot alien hogs and signal to Joss or Sterling.

Not one of the herders signaled the boys this time, on their return, that they had spotted an underbit.

"Let's take smack down the middle this time," Joss suggested. "You get over from me about two yards."

Because Tobias's mark was the overbit—a slice into the top of the right ear—it was usually easy to spot and pass over. The hogs here belonging to Hank's family bore the crop mark, which was also easy to spot. Sometimes, from the position a hog's head was turned, the boys failed to see the overbit or the crop and hopefully pushed closer. But a change in position, of either hog or boy, would quickly reveal to them their error, and they would move on, shoving disappointment aside.

134

"There!" They said it in unison, each spotting the same two hogs at the same time. They were in a cluster of Durocs, their dust-blanketed backs appearing no darker than those about them, though actually their half-breed color was a red-black.

To the brush of meal under their snouts, the underbits paid no heed. They had found some camas root and were rooting eagerly into the soil.

Joss frowned. "Let's try roping 'em away, then the feed."

It was a simple job to slip nooses over groveling heads and under front legs. Pulling them away was another matter. Sterling's captive crashed sideways, snorting furiously, knocking Sterling's knees from under him. He catapulted into the dirt. The hog, still looped with the rope, stood back and stared, its eyes dazed. Joss's hog squealed its annoyance and leaped stright, shooting out of the rope like a bullet.

Two more attempts, as futile, brought Tobias's wrath down upon them in raging insults.

"Fools! Fools!" he screamed from his position at the feed wagon. "You've wasted half the rest time! I'll give you five more minutes, then the underbits are mine! I've waited too long, too long!"

Joss's face was one mass of streaked mud, and behind the mud, the shade of burnt brick. He paused and glared at his tormentor. "For every one of mine you get, you

old horned toad," he muttered under his breath, "I'll have one of yours."

"Try the meal again, now," Joss said to Sterling. They had discarded the bucket for pockets, and now dipped in to fill their palms.

The hogs were so distracted, now, that they forgot

what it was they were rooting for and took after the meal-caked hands with surprising suddenness. It kept the boys sprinting in and around the herd to keep ahead.

Hank met them as they broke out of the herd. He had been maneuvering out, too, one underbit in anxious pursuit of his meal-covered hand.

"Obliged, Hank," Joss said. "That leaves one. Take these back, Sterl. I'll find the other one."

"Just one matter much, Joss?" Hank asked. "Ain't seventy-one enough?"

"I need every last one," Joss declared, his jaws clamping in determination. He pivoted back into the herd.

Joss knew his lone hog had to be somewhere in the inside of the herd, and most likely up toward the front. The herders would have spotted it, otherwise, circling constantly as they were.

His eyes, flitting from one pair of ears to another, sometimes moved ahead of his brain and he had to backtrack to let his thinking catch up. "Underbit," he caught himself mumbling in a daze, after skimming over twenty or thirty hogs. "Underbit," he would say; then, "No underbit." Then he could go on.

He was up toward the front now, still going, still checking, and wondering, with another part of his mind, why Tobias hadn't called time. It seemed like a half a century since Tobias had barked out the five-minute time limit.

And then he saw his hog. Most of its body was hidden

137

by a sage bush. It was lying down, facing him, over to his left four paces. Its body was black up past the belly, where it had been standing in the stream. Its eyes were closed, but the underbit showed plainly.

Joss felt the thrill of his find go through him. He had them all now, all seventy-two!

He sprang toward the animal, knowing he had less than seconds to spare.

Even as he covered the four yards, Tobias shrilled, "Time's up!"

"Come, pig! Come, pig pig," Joss coaxed urgently, brushing the still snout with his meal-caked hand. He shook the sleeping head gently.

"Get out, Joss! Leave at once! I'm through waiting!" The voice was commanding and sharp. It pierced through Joss like knives.

"Come, pig pig," Joss urged desperately. "Wake up. Come, pig."

The hog stirred slightly, rumbled deep in its throat, then settled back down.

Joss shook the big slumbering head again, more violently. "Up, pig!" he shouted. "Wake up, pig! Come, pig pig!"

Joss glanced up and saw that Tobias was swinging toward him through the flock. His stride was long, ground-covering, and angry.

Joss stood up and faced him, waited for him to come

138

closer. He could see the dark wrath in Tobias's face. He had always known that Tobias meant business. Now he felt it clear to his marrow. Tobias held an open knife in his hand, the kind used for slitting the ears of hogs. He was coming to make good his threat.

Joss planted his feet squarely in front of his dozing hog, between it and Tobias, and waited.

"I need this hog, Tobias," Joss sang out, when Tobias was twenty feet away. "I need it bad. Call your hogs to feed. I won't let this one follow, even if it wants to."

In the flash of time that it took Tobias to cross the gap between them, Joss felt surprise at the strong way he moved. He had always thought of him as being small and gangly.

Tobias was before Joss, now. He reached out a hand, clutched Joss's shoulder, and swept him aside. Then he was down on his knees, his knife blade flashing into the tip of the hog's right ear. He had uttered no word since his arrival.

Joss's face was no longer the shade of baked red brick, but a dirty and clammy ash gray. His hands grasped a round river rock, the size of a musk-melon. He dropped it, now, full force, on the head of the hog, just as the shock of the cut brought the hog squawking out of slumber. It sank to the ground again, the sounds dying in its throat.

"You like dead hogs, Tobias?" Joss asked, his voice

almost a whisper. "You got one." He turned and walked out of the herd. He looked no place but directly in front of him.

Tobias was standing, gaping after Joss. Once his head swerved to stare at the dead hog. Once his mouth opened to call after the boy. But it closed again. He watched in silence as Joss strode up the slope. When he was gone Tobias called to a herder.

"Butcher it," he instructed. "We'll eat it. You others get out the feed. Time to feed." He walked back to his wagon.

Two hours later one of Tobias's herders found the boys lying on the creek bank. The underbits were dozing or moving idly about.

"Time to march," the herder announced.

Joss sat up and searched the herder's face. "Tobias say we could come?"

"He sent me back to tell ye," the herder said. He laughed as he turned away. He laughed softly all the way out of Joss's hearing.

Joss studied the herder's back as he retreated, his face puzzled. Then he said, "Let's roll," and began to hitch up the team. It was his stint at the wagon, now, Sterling's with the hogs.

When he had the team going at a slow pace, Joss turned and called:

"Here, pig pig! Come, pig pig!"

The hogs looked toward him as one and moved in his direction.

"Suffering sidewinders!" Joss breathed to himself. Some cabbagehead he was. Why hadn't he thought of that this morning, or would they have understood, then, that to follow the wagon meant food?

Two herds joined them before dark. Each time, Joss paused to the rear a good hundred yards and waited till the last of the new herd was almost out of sight before starting the team.

His own hogs moved close, now.

"This is easy as apple pie, Joss!" Sterling called once, and grinned.

Joss returned the grin, but only quickly. The grim lines that had been there ever since he had killed his own hog returned. Even if it was apple pie easy all the way, they still could be just one hog short of five hundred dollars.

They camped that night long after dark. The boys didn't know how long after, or what time it was. All they knew was that the moon was halfway up the velvet sky and that they became accustomed to seeing by moonlight; it was almost like a dark, shaded day. They realized the wisdom of driving at this time: the air was cool and damp, it settled the dust. The hogs were not apt to collapse from heat and motion. They were in the mood for moving now, had gotten the feel of it, were rested and fed.

Joss got a fire going. Sterling watched the hogs at the creek, then broke out some corn from the wagon.

When the coals were low Joss tossed four potatoes into the embers. He laced slices of salt pork onto willow switches and hung them low over the coals. That, and fresh plums, somewhat mauled from the day's journey, was their meal.

The boys' eyes were heavy as they banked the fire and took a last survey of the herd. The hogs were down already, quiet and sleeping.

"I'll sleep on the other side of the herd," Joss said, yawning, pulling a blanket from the wagon. "You better stay here. We can see things better like that. G'night."

Joss received one good face-up view of the moon, bobbing brilliantly over his head, when his eyes blinked shut and stayed that way.

But even so, Joss did not rest. He tossed and twisted and flung off his blanket, only to reach out for it when his chilled body came half awake. Many pictures danced before his dream-filled mind. Some made him cry out, like the one where he killed the hog. Some made him sick, deep inside, like his father saying, "I'll be ready to go back East when you get back," and an even deeper

142

sickness when Pop bobbed up in his dream and said, "Sometimes a man has to be hog wild."

Once during the night he woke himself out of his own dreams with his cries. It startled him into wide-awakeness. He flung the wetness from his eyes and pulled the blanket back around him. He'd been calling for Firetop. He remembered, now, as he snuggled back down into the blanket. He'd been calling and calling, pleading for the collie to come.

But that was silly, he scolded himself, now that he was awake and in his right mind. Toppy was safe at home.

He burrowed deeper into the blanket and told himself to go back to sleep. Tomorrow would be a long day.

Chapter 13

Parting Company

For no reason that he could think of, then or later, Joss woke suddenly and completely an hour before dawn. The moon winked at him through the gnarly branches of a thorn bush. The morning was clear, moonswept, and cold. He sat up, stuffed his feet into his boots—the only apparel he had removed—stood up and shook his blanket and rolled it into a bundle.

As he rounded the herd toward the wagon he noticed that some of his hogs were up and moving about.

In minutes the fire blazed high round two chunks of dried wood.

Sterling stumbled groggily out of his blanket and on down to the creek. "Only the shock of water will revive me," he muttered.

Joss cooked wheat cereal and topped it with thick slices of ham and butter. "Got to finish these plums, too," he said, passing a handful to Sterling. "They're getting squishy as mud."

Sterling bit into the fruit obediently.

"Two things just don't make sense to me, Joss."

"Like?"

"Well, I know Tobias doesn't like us, but it doesn't seem like that would be his reason for putting us at the tail of the drive, when we started in second place."

"I got that figured, Sterl. He wants unsquashed browse for his hogs, see, when he stops at rest time and night, figures his hogs won't lose so much travel weight if they get the best feed off the land like that. More pennies to jingle or stick up his nose or whatever he does with 'em."

Sterling laughed. "He probably has a Midas room, counts his coins punctually at ten every morning. Well, that answers the second question—why the separation —but I still don't understand why we have to be at the tail, eating everyone else's dust."

"Mostly because we're younguns, I'd say. We can't talk back, or shouldn't. Leastways it'd be kind of unhandy at this distance. It's a sure thing he don't cotton to us. Probably just wants us as far away as possible."

Sterling washed dishes while Joss hooked up the team and got the wagon balanced to travel. A campfire, still

145

blazing at the camp ahead, told the boys that they were early.

"Probably better count hogs before we start," Joss said. "Got some rocks?"

"I will have in a jiffy. I dumped them out last night when I retired."

"Here." Joss handed over a fistful. "Don't know how this'll work, but we can try it. I'll stand between the wagon and that tree, and call. I'll give 'em a push by me when they lick my hand. You stand at the corner of the wagon and call, and push 'em on around. We'll spread a little meal back there to make 'em think they got something for a couple shakes."

They got ready, then Joss called, not too loudly.

Sterling shoved as the hogs came forth, and, for every five, dropped one pebble into his empty pocket.

Finally Joss said, "Whew! That's it, I guess. How's the count?"

"Something is wrong, Joss. I must have made a mistake. I came out even. I should have had one extra, for seventy-one."

"How many fives?"

Sterling carefully extracted the rocks and counted.

"Fourteen."

Joss searched the spot where the hogs had bedded down. It was open and empty, except for a mauled sage

146

here and there, a thorn bush too thin to conceal a hog behind.

"We'll count over," Joss decided. His features resumed the grim lines that the night had almost erased.

"I think we should," Sterling agreed. "It's probably just my mistake."

They finished counting as Tobias's herder appeared and told them to be ready to march in a matter of minutes.

Joss ended the count with fourteen rocks even. He frowned. "Same as you, Sterl."

"You fellers got troubles?" The herder paused before swinging back on his path.

"We're shy a hog," Joss said. "Thanks for coming back."

"Better not wait to find your stray," the herder advised. "Get too far behind. Might have wandered into the bunch up ahead."

"We'll have a look around. We'll catch you. Much oblige."

The boys decided that Sterling would keep watch at camp while Joss scoured out in all directions.

He went downstream first, toward the other herds. He hurdled logs and pressed through sparse thickets of service and thorn, calling "pig pig" now and then. His eyes ferreted into the shaded bushy spots. If not satisfied

147

with the answer of his vision, he would go there bodily.

He reached the wagon ahead as it was beginning to move out. He asked the driver if he had noticed a stray hog, one with an underbit mark. The man said he hadn't seen one, but told Joss to have a look around anyway. Joss thanked him and looked, circling the small sea of Poland-Chinas. He walked through the herd, searching, but finding no mark but the halfcrop. He thanked the man again and swung back.

He returned by way of the hillside, climbing to a new height on the slope, calling, peering, gouging into bushes, searching thickets. He reached the wagon with a find of absolute zero.

"I've been wondering about that thicket," Sterling said, gesturing upstream and across.

"I been eyeing that," Joss said, "though why in tarnation one hog would get interested in that bramble patch I don't see. I'll go look for tracks leading out of the water."

Seconds later: "Tracks are here, Sterl! I bet it's one of them canyon hogs, thinking it's found its home. I'll figure to hurry."

He found a deer trail at one end of the gorge and scrambled up it, calling "pig pig!" from breathless lungs.

He had not climbed twenty feet when an uproar started, off to his left. Bushes began smashing and crash-

148

ing, as if a huge boulder from someplace on top had been loosed and was thrashing its way to a standstill far below.

Even as Joss jumped back against the canyon wall, his ears picked up grunting sounds, squealing, protesting sounds! His stray hog!

But what? What was it doing to create such an upheaval of noise? Had it loosed an avalanche of rock? Had something attacked it?

The sound was going down, now, receding out of the canyon.

Joss faced back downtrail. He burst out of the thicket at the same moment that the hog shot forth, bolting down across the rocky embankment that separated the creek from the canyon. And what was this?

"No! No!" Joss cried under his breath. "No, Toppy, no!"

But it was Firetop, his fire-red body doubling and stretching, rocketing at breakneck speed only inches behind the streaking, squeaking hog.

Then Joss laughed. He collapsed on the ground and laughed so hard and big at first that the sound could hardly escape from his throat. He choked and beat the ground with his fists and sobbed and laughed.

Firetop paused at the creek bank and watched till the hog had leaped the stream and bolted into the protection of the herd. Then he turned toward Joss. He swung his head just a little, wagged his tail like he would shake it off, and sidled forward with tiny mincing steps.

"Black as sin, aren't you, Top?" Joss cried, his face wet and wrinkled with the effort of talking. "Black as sin. Bad Toppy."

A soft, low whine started deep in Firetop's throat. Then, as if he couldn't stand it any longer, he sprang forward. He lit on top of Joss, bowling him over, nosing into his neck, rolling with him on the rocky ground.

Later when Joss was running loving hands over Firetop's big, furry body, he said, "Guess you know what a fix you got me in; guess you know I'm going to have to send you home."

Suddenly, the hand that had been stroking down the collie's weak thigh and leg, stopped. Joss's startled eyes darted down to check on what his hand had discovered.

"What in tarnation—" Joss mumbled in alarm. "Toppy, what—you got a foot, Top!" he marveled.

Sterling had waded the creek and was now beside Joss and his dog, staring as Joss had stared, amazement as awash on his features. Then he ventured, "It looks to me like Ropejon has been pretty busy since we left yesterday morning, to have come up with a padded pegleg like that."

"Who'd ever've thought of a padded pegleg 'cepting Ropejon, Sterl! Stand up, Toppy. Let's see how it fits with your weight on it."

150

Firetop obediently gained all four feet and stalked about. He limped only slightly.

"Good dog, Top! Come here now, lay down. Oh, yes, you're tops all right. Now let's see what makes the limp, 'cepting what's in your head."

Joss discovered that the pegleg was laced with fine cuttings of leather and resembled a boot more than a peg. He unlaced the boot and slipped it off.

"Lookit there, Sterl. It even has a pillow inside!"

"Ropejon is really an artist," Sterling praised, examining the boot.

Joss was pressing on the stump of Firetop's leg. "Funny kind of crazy old Ropejon is. Probably people got to saying that because he's just plumb too smart, and they couldn't tell the difference, not being used to either one."

Firetop drew his leg back, wincing just a little.

"A mite sore, isn't it, Top? Well, it's boundin' to be, right at first. You kind of got to get calloused up, see. Ropejon thought he was helping, thought we'd need you, and we do, too, only we can't have you. We got to get to Prairie Town as best we can, without any more fuss that we can help. I hate like sin to send you home, Top, but that's just the way it is. So come on, now. We'll get your boot on. Your stump won't get too sore on the way back. You can favor it some."

Joss slipped the boot back in place, laced and tied it.

151

"Okay, Top, goodbye, feller. Go home, now. Tell Ropejon that's a first-rate boot. 'Bye, Toppy."

Firetop lowered his head to the ground. He scratched an ear with a front paw. He angled his eyes up at Joss. He made no pretense at getting up.

"I know you don't want to go," Joss said, ruffling the dog's head. "But you got to, Top. I'm way behind now. We'll hurry back home. Go now. Go home, Toppy."

The collie uttered a long, drawnout, emptying sigh. He almost closed his eyes in boredom before lifting them, somewhat blandly, to his master. His body hadn't moved.

Joss rammed his fists into pockets and stared off across the prairie. "If I took him home, we'd lose a day, even if I could take him home. He's so tarnation set on going with us."

Sterling was thoughtful, too. "Suppose we just told Tobias that Firetop has joined us, and that we'll keep a mile or so behind so we can't be any bother to him at all."

"I don't think it would work, Sterl. Tobias wouldn't cotton to it, and I wouldn't, either, not with that mad sow up there someplace. No, I got to take him back. You wait here. I'll try to be back by dark. We can drive a long time after that, like last night."

They went back across the creek, with Firetop at their

heels, jumping from stone to stone, as if purposely trying to keep his boot dry.

"Wonder what Hank's coming this way for?" Joss said, his eyes turned north.

Joss went to the wagon and got out some dried prunes to chew on, on the way home. He found a piece of bread and offered it to Firetop.

The dog sniffed at it and turned away. "Ropejon stuffed you up good, didn't he, you stubborn old idiot?"

Hank came up, said "howdy," and asked why they hadn't started yet, even though he saw the collie, knowing that he was a recent and sure-trouble addition.

"We're parking here today," Joss said sourly. "I got to take Top back home. You on friendly inspection for your boss?"

Hank spat out away from him as far as possible, as if the very mention of Tobias put a foul taste in his mouth.

"He ain't my boss, Joss. Not any more."

Joss stared at Hank. "What do you mean, he ain't your boss?"

"Just that. I quit. I quit old skinflint. You know what he had the gall to do? You know that cantankerous sow of his. Well, she wandered out during the night sometime. So here comes skinflint and tells me to find that sow. 'Find 'er yourself,' I says. I'm not about to get myself mauled from that hog."

Joss was becoming more worried by the minute, even while wondering just how much of Hank's talk was hot air. You could never tell by listening to him. Still, he had quit his job.

"So you're going home now, Hank?"

"Nope, not by a jugful. I stopped to ask you for a job. I'll help you clean to Prairie Town and charge you only four cartwheels, same as old skinflint was paying me. What do you say?"

Joss didn't know what to say. Hank was a friend and all that. And here was a solution to his immediate problem—Hank and Sterling could drive the hogs while he took Toppy home. But then there was the money problem. He would still make it, barely, if the prices stayed at two and a half cents, and if the hogs didn't lose too much weight on the drive. But if the price went down, even a fraction of a cent, or he lost more hogs, or some of them lost weight—

"Much obliged for the offer, Hank, but I don't know if I'll have four dollars to spare. I got to end up with five hundred, you know."

"Well then, tell ya what I'll do, Joss. I'll just sign up with ya, and if you ain't got your five hundred you won't have to pay me, now. Pay me, say, next year, when you get the money."

Joss thought that over. That would be all right, wouldn't it? What could it hurt?

"Okay, Hank, it's a bargain. I'll pay you in Prairie Town, if the sale comes to over five hundred dollars. If it don't, I'll pay you when I can, not later than at hog drive time next year."

"You got yourself a hand, boss."

Joss swacked him in the ribs. "Okay, you two. Get the herd down the line. I'll catch up with you sometime between now and morning."

Joss started up the sloping backtrail on the run. "Okay, stubborn Toppy, come on home."

The dog ran with his master until they were well started, away from the herd. His tail wagged happily. Then, abruptly, the collie slowed down, turned, glanced back at the herd below him and the wagon that had begun to move. He swung back and looked at Joss, still running on, calling and whistling to him.

Firetop came to a dead stop. He sat on his haunches in the middle of the road and stared at his master.

"Come on, Toppy. Let's go home, dog!" Joss coaxed, slowing, but still moving up the road.

Firetop whined deep in this throat but refused to budge a muscle.

Joss came back and talked to the dog, explaining again why he couldn't go, promising to take him next year on the drive, pleading with him to be a good dog and come along now without any more fuss.

Firetop answered by coming to his feet, dashing back

155

downtrail in the direction of the slowly moving hogs, swinging around, barking, swinging back again, going on.

Then Joss lost his temper. He called his dog every name that ranch-hand lore had taught him. He invited the devil to come and whisk him away and roast him over his hottest flames. He accused Firetop of dropping every ounce of sense he owned when he left home. He abused and insulted and raved, pausing only to see what effect his words were having.

At times Firetop would hang his head, his tail brushing the ground. At other times he would perch on his haunches and howl back, his eyes rolling nervously. Sometimes he would stand taut and still, his ears straight, his head alert, as if striving to catch every inflection of Joss's voice. He stayed his distance, reacting in different ways to the boy's temper, but overall, waiting, watching, as if biding his time until Joss cooled down.

And eventually Joss's streams of wrath subsided. He collapsed to the ground, spent of anger and strength, his face white and sponged in sweat. He took his head in his hands and gulped air into his lungs. When Firetop came close and nudged his nose into Joss's spread fingers, Joss lifted a limp hand and hung it across the dog's neck.

After a while he said, his voice weak, "How come you're so tarnation stubborn?"

As if that were an invitation for romp and merriment, Firetop began to wriggle all over, making whining noises, his mouth nosing in to swack Joss a few licks on the face and neck.

"I don't know," Joss sighed, refusing the offer to play. "I sure don't know what to do with you."

Only one possible thing, now. Hold up the hogs. Tell Tobias what happened and get out of his drive. Follow along behind in a day or two. He didn't know how it was going to work out, either. What if he got to Prairie Town too late, after the buyers were gone? What if the buyers would see that he was just a punk and only offer him two cents? Maybe that was what Pop had been concerned over when he had insisted that he go with Tobias. Still, he couldn't go with Tobias. Not now.

Joss rose and walked down the road toward his hogs and wagon. They were a quarter mile distant. He picked up speed. He would have to get them stopped.

Firetop bolted ahead, as if seeing something, way down there, that required his immediate attention.

Joss called to Hank, explained the new situation. "I'll get along up and tell Tobias," he added. "We'll let the hogs spread now. Top can bring 'em in when we want 'em close."

When Joss told the collie to stay with the hogs, he half expected him to refuse, but in this he was wrong. Without a moment's hesitation, the dog trotted back and around the herd.

157

It took Joss about an hour to reach Tobias's wagon. Another herd had joined the drive. That made four wagons and about six acres of hogs. That was a lot of hogs to come in behind, at Prairie Town.

Joss came up to Tobias, walked alongside, and stated his business. "Much oblige, anyway," he ended. "I'll be trailing in probably two days behind."

Tobias sat up a little straighter on his wagon seat. He didn't look at Joss.

"You can't do that," he snapped. "I made an agreement with your pa. You're coming along. Just stay back a quarter mile."

This was such an unexpected reaction from Tobias that it caught Joss completely off-track. He'd let him come along! He wouldn't have to drag in two days behind! These thoughts took hold of him for a number of seconds. Then he thought of the mad sow, and everything went bad again. A quarter mile, or even a whole, wasn't too far for that sow to wander.

Joss swallowed on a lump that stuck in his throat. "I can't, Tobias. I can't, that's all. I'll follow in two days. Much obliged anyway."

"You're muley," Tobias stated, his voice clapping sharp and angry. "Always will be. All right then, go it alone. I'm not responsible for you after this minute."

"G'bye, Tobias."

Tobias didn't answer.

158

Joss swung back. He was almost numb with the sick feelings he had inside. He could not help but ask himself:

Will we get enough money if we wait? If we don't, then Pop—but if I do go along, then Top might get mauled again. Funny how he wasn't mad at Firetop anymore. He was so mixed up—

It was along toward evening. The boys had played in the ice-cold creek, had munched on dried fruit and bread, whittled whistles and charms, and told whopping fibs. They sprawled on backs and sides, dreamily soaking in the last rays of a setting sun.

Suddenly Hank bolted up to a sitting position. He stared at Joss as if he hadn't seen him for a year. "We don't have to wait, Joss!" he declared. "By geecracks, we can leave tonight! Right now!"

Joss took another, unhurried bite out of an apple. "What are you talking about?"

"A short cut, lad! It just come to me! I was over it with old Ward Houston two years ago. It takes you down over the prairie more in a beeline than the road. It cuts corners and big loopouts that the road hangs to. Beat old skinflint to Prairie Town by two days! What do you say, boss?"

Joss rolled over on his stomach. He rubbed his chin on the pebbly ground and considered. He forced excitement away from his thoughts. This wasn't a time to start

159

out on a hog wild notion, just maybe from a hot air say-so from Hank.

"How do you get on to this here short cut?" Joss inquired.

"Right now, right here! We know Prairie Town's northwest, don't we?"

"Okay. So what?"

"So, we just get us a marker that says by the setting sun that it's clean northwest. Then head for it. Simple. Bye and bye we'll reach the Clearwater, cross it, and climb to the top of the prairie again. Then we're bound to bump into the stage road that leads into Prairie Town. Nothing to it, boss!"

Joss raised his head to gaze at the many endless, rolling hills out to the north and west. They all looked alike—mile after mile of humped, slightly descending terrain. Due north, the hills were higher, shutting out what lay beyond. This was the way the stage road went, the way Tobias had gone.

"Why don't Tobias take the short cut, then, Hank, if it's so all-fired shorter and better?"

"He wouldn't get to pick up other bunches along the way. See, he deals with a buyer for so many hundreds of hogs. That way the price is highest, because a buyer comes on a certain date, see, with so many empty railroad cars. It saves time and fooling around. And that saves money. Knowing Tobias, that's all I have to say, ain't it?"

"Yep." Joss sat up to face Hank. "You mean if I hold up here for two days, drag in after Tobias, the price might be dropped, the cars gone, nobody to take my hogs, or pay me?" Joss studied Hank's face for signs of story-telling.

"I couldn't say about that," Hank answered seriously. "Maybe. Maybe not. Oh, there'd be somebody there prob-ably, to take the hogs off your hands, but you might not get as much out of 'em as if you went in the same time as Tobias. Probably wouldn't be best to go in ahead of him, at that."

Joss felt that Hank was on the square. And that ex-plained why Tobias wanted him along, even if it meant putting up with Toppy. He'd bargained with a dealer for so many and was afraid the lower amount might mean a lower price.

"We'd want to get there about when Tobias got there," Joss said, thinking out loud.

"Right," Hank said.

"And what about the wagon?" Sterling asked. "Will it make it over those hills, where there isn't a road?"

"Ward Houston made it," Hank declared. "The pace is so slow the driver has time to pick out a easy way."

"What about water?" Joss queried.

"There's little springs and creeks all over. Just like

161

home, Joss. You know how it is there."

The excitement that Joss had been resolutely pushing away while he examined the idea for flaws now began to creep in. They'd be free of the mad sow; they had Firetop; Hank knew the country, or acted mighty like he did; they'd have time to take it slow. What could be hog wild about it?

Joss came to his feet in one leap. He hitched up his pants and grinned at his cousin.

He asked of Hank, "How many miles do you figure we can cover by midnight?"

Hank delivered a swat to Joss's back. "Plenty, boss! Plenty enough!"

They slapped each other and jostled about, the thrill of going it alone bubbling out of them.

Sterling offered to take first stint at the wagon.

In less than ten minutes they were underway. Then Joss remembered Firetop's tender stump and paused long enough to remove the boot for the rest of the evening.

Joss hummed a tune, then whistled, then hummed, as he traveled the outside of the herd.

He was getting his dream wish, one that he hadn't even dared to mention to Pop. He was going it alone, without Tobias, because it seemed the best solution.

And it wasn't so far, not really, to Prairie Town. Just eighty or so miles over these hills.

Chapter 14

The Short Cut

The high peak in the distance, which the boys had chosen before dark as their guidepost, stood out in bright silhouette against the moonlit sky. As the fat, round moon winked and blinked its way through the heavens, it seemed headed directly for the high peak. But then, as it crossed the top of the velvet sky, Joss saw that it was turning away, heading west. That was good. That meant that they were on course, so far.

Hank and Joss walked with the herd on either side, sometimes passing each other on their rounds.

Joss tried yodeling, like he'd heard a man do once, but decided to quit when Firetop dashed up, whining nervously.

Joss was preparing to skirt a clump of willows when

it occurred to him that here was a possibility of water. He investigated and found a pool, shallow and wide. He checked with the moon, found it to be slightly west of his head, and decided it was time to call a stop. He notified Sterling and found buckets to dip some clear water before the hogs got to it.

Sterling freed the horses while Hank got a fire going. Joss rummaged into the food box to see what to cook. Firetop headed the hogs in toward the spring.

Joss decided on roasted potatoes again, and scrambled eggs. He dropped two extra eggs into the pan and tried the extra portion on the collie. He had stirred into it shavings of jerky and bread and butter. Firetop licked the pan clean.

He couldn't do this all the time, though—feed two extra mouths that food hadn't been provided for. He could buy food in Prairie Town, if he had any extra money, but that was a big 'if.'

Except for the worry about adequate food supplies, Joss was in good spirits, and joined the other two in telling after-dinner tales. Hank had been making up to Sterling, and now asked him about New York, and what he did for fun.

Sterling replied that he was left alone quite a bit of the time, except for a housekeeper. His mother, he told Hank, had died several years before. Since that time it had been rather sad at home, although his father was always trying to make things cheerful.

"How come you to never learn to catch a ball, Sterl?" Hank asked.

"Oh, I never was good at things like that," Sterling answered, his expression thoughtful. "Maybe it's because I started late, trying to. I was never as good as the others, though. I found that out real fast. I found also that no one wants a poor player on his side, so I just quit. I'm just not good at things like that."

"Awww!" Joss denied, squinting into the dying flames. "Look how you handle the lasso!"

"Yeah," Hank agreed. "I'd like to've seen that roping you did that first day of the drive. Joss was telling me. I don't know anybody as can rope a hog."

"It was probably just luck," Sterling said. "And the riata, of course."

"Sterl, you plumb peeve me," Joss snorted. "You shouldn't ought to talk that way, always making yourself look so small."

"I'm sorry, Joss," Sterling apologized, making Joss feel even more annoyed.

Joss came to his feet. "I'm hitting the hay," he announced in disgusted tones. He didn't feel disgusted, though, not really. He wanted to spur Sterling into feeling differently about himself. But Hank was too close. He didn't feel right talking so personal, with outsiders close.

Hank stood and yawned. "If I get my four cartwheels when we hit Prairie Town, I'm going to buy the biggest plate of oysters in town for four bits. You guys ever et a oyster dinner?"

Sterling nodded without comment. He was banking the fire.

Joss said he never had, that he could remember.

"Oysters!" Hank moaned, longingly. "That's what most of the punk herders live for on these here drives —just to get to Prairie Town and eat up their cartwheels on oysters. I guess the hotels must order up a whole extra barrel of oysters at hog drive time."

"Have to try that," Joss commented, "if hogs is up to three cents."

"I heard someplace that the price was up to three 'n' a half," Hank remarked. "Heard that's what Tobias was agreed on."

"If that's so, then I'll stake you to a plate of oysters," Joss promised.

All three boys crossed to the wagon to find their blankets. Minutes later the only sound around the camp was an occasional snapping of a coal.

It seemed only minutes to Joss when Firetop's low, warning growl brought him up from deep sleep.

He blinked into the dawn air and saw three white-tail deer just above them on the hill. They were standing

166

still, eyeing this strange trespass of their domain.

Joss had shot his first deer the year before. He knew where to aim. He cautioned Firetop to silence and crept toward the wagon for the thirty-thirty. He had extracted the gun from its sheath and was bringing it up for aim, when Hank woke.

"Daylight!" Hank yelped. "Daylight, guys! Roll out!" He was already thrashing off his blanket.

The three animals on the slope turned as one and loped away. Joss blessed Hank with some of his choice names and let go with the best aim he knew he would get.

The deer that was farthest behind fell without a sound. It rolled backward down the hill.

Hank had barged to his feet and was glaring around wild-eyed.

Sterling was standing, his eyes wide on Joss.

"That's not oysters, fellers," Joss said, a grin splitting his face, "but it'll sure fill the holes in your bellies."

All three helped gut the animal and string it to a cottonwood. Hank and Joss skinned the carcass. Sterling tended to building up the fire.

They decided that even the liver was too fresh to eat, and placed it and the heart in a pail of water to cool out.

After breakfast the meat was strapped to the wagon rack so that the air would get to it. When the sun warmed the air the boys would cover the vension with a piece of canvas.

"Now you'll be getting plenty of dog meat, Top," Joss assured him as he fastened the peg-boot onto the collie's leg.

Joss took the team and rolled out, heading straight for the peak.

They descended into a wide, small valley, climbed, descended again, took their time until the sun beat down hot and penetrating.

A noisy, bubbly stream, cascading down a rock bluff, became their noonday camp spot.

The boys broke out sacks of wheat and corn and spread the contents over the ground. Joss observed his hogs as they lined up to drink. They still look fat and sleek, he thought.

Joss fried liver and heart for the noon meal and doled out bread and apples.

The sun was hot. Firetop was watching the hogs. The horses chewed placidly. The boys dozed in comfort, with a sense of well-being.

When they woke they found that the air had turned chill. The sun no longer beat an unobstructed path to the earth. Clouds were before it, hazy, cottony, a netting of gray-white.

"Good driving weather, Joss," Hank said. "Hogs don't get so hot, not so liable to sunstroke. You can drive longer."

168

"Let's get to 'er then," Joss said. "Quit earlier to-night."

It was Hank's turn at the wagon. The horses plodded along at their usual pace. Hank fell to wondering and dreaming and wishing; wishing Joss would have enough to pay him; dreaming about the boots he would buy, and the oysters; wondering if he would see the pretty girl he saw last year—

The sky grew darker. The air became more chilled.

Joss walked at the rear of the herd. His eyes were constantly alert, noting the condition of a hog that strayed or lagged behind. These truants always received his careful examination. So far none were breaking down in the back, like he had heard many hogs did when traveling to Prairie Town. The stubblefields had been good training ground. Still, it paid to watch.

Much later Joss raised his eyes to check on the landmark. Alarm shot through him. The landmark wasn't there!

His startled eyes raced from right to left of the wagon. The wagon was moving steadily forward, as if Hank knew just where he were going.

But how could he? There was nothing, absolutely nothing out there but a dark and purpling overcast.

Sterling came up beside Joss and walked with him a few strides.

"Does he know where he's going, Sterl?"

"I have been wondering. I don't see how he could know."

"I got to go see, Sterl." Joss left Sterling on the run, circling the herd.

About the time that Joss decided to investigate Hank's driving, Hank came out of his daydreaming. He checked for his landmark and found it missing. He glanced around in blank dismay for a second or so, then threw an uncertain glance back over his shoulder. He saw Joss coming up on the run.

He secured a more firm hold on the reins and tried to squint through the banks of purple clouds to the hills that he knew lay beyond. They must be straight out the way they were going, he reasoned. The horses couldn't have drawn away too much to right or left. His grin to Joss was full of assurance.

"I got a bead on 'er, boss. Odd, ain't it, how you can sense you're going in the right direction, even if you can't tell with your eyes?"

Joss eyed Hank's calm and confident face. "Maybe we should stop. We got plenty of time, you said. Maybe this'll blow over by morning."

"Why, Joss?" Hank managed a look of superiority. "Didn't I tell ya this was the best driving weather? Might be we'll need them two extra days up the way a spell. We best use this good weather while we got it."

170

One thing, Joss thought, was good: they were going steadily downhill, and that was as it should be. They'd go down now till they reached the Clearwater. They couldn't go too far wrong if they just kept heading downhill.

"Go ahead," Joss said, and turned back to the herd.

Soon after Joss reached his position at the rear of the hogs, faint sounds of thunder reached his ears. At first it was off to the north, distant and harmless. The hogs heard it, too. They raised their heads to listen, stopping in their tracks.

It was so dark now that the hogs farthest from Joss looked like a cloudy blur, almost as if the muddled sky had dropped before him on the ground, rumbling and uneasy.

When the first thin ribbon of lightning cut the sky to the north, Joss knew that they were in for a first-class prairie storm. He sprinted around the right of the herd, toward where he had last seen Sterling.

"We're stopping now, Sterl," he gasped, rushing up. "Come on with me. You might get trampled in a stampede here."

Sterling fell in behind Joss, who was already racing on toward the wagon.

Crack! That was closer!

Joss reached the wagon in long bounds.

"Stop, Hank, stop! Whoa! Sugar, Old Priss!"

"What's the matter?" Hank's voice sounded in the darkness. "You going to let a little storm slow you up?"

"You bet. This one'll slow us up real smart."

Joss let out a whistle that was meant for Firetop alone. In seconds the dog was there, nudging Joss's legs, panting loudly.

And then the sky broke loose. It cracked like a fallen Humpty Dumpty, each jagged section fringed in forked lightning, each piece bemoaning the rent.

The hog herd exploded, too. In one mammoth, collective, grunting response, the fear-crazed animals spanged out in all directions, as if each one, individually, was stabbed in the rump with a pitchfork.

Joss had freed the team, in case the wagon was tipped over by the maddened hogs. He acted from a plan he carried in his mind for just such an emergency.

The boys stood between the horses and the wagon. The horses faced them, whinnying softly, but not attempting escape.

The hogs bolted and hurtled by, missing them only by feet, and missing them that much only because the wagon, at the point of the drive, had parted them.

In only seconds they were gone, completely swallowed up in the black night.

The sky continued its display of fireworks, clapping loud at its own artistry.

In spite of himself, Joss held his breath, waiting for

173

the next act. He had seen many lightning storms such as this; they were a common occurrence on the prairie after a long dry spell. Still, it was big and mighty, and seemed almost to smite their very noses with its wonderful, engulfing wrath.

When it was over—and it ended quickly, in a matter of minutes—Joss gulped air into his starving lungs. "Whew!" he coughed. "That was a show!" The others agreed in chastened tones.

Nothing to do now but camp here till morning. Not a drop of rain had fallen. They couldn't see a foot in front of their faces. Dawn would have to light the way to water. Joss only hoped that none of the hogs had injured itself in its raving hurry to escape the storm. Firetop would bring them in.

Joss passed out apples and the last of the bread.

Minutes later they were rolled up in their blankets, side by side.

Joss reached out to give Firetop a goodnight pat. "I suppose if you could talk you'd be telling me you knew all about that storm coming, and that's why you wouldn't go home, knowing we'd never round up all them hogs without you."

The collie's response was a wet lick on Joss's wrist.

Joss's last thoughts were of Tobias. He had no dog to round up his stampeded hogs. He'd be late to Prairie Town, too. That should have been all right, but, for

174

some reason, the fact that Tobias would be late caused Joss to feel uneasy. It came to him, sometime during his fitful night of sleep, just why this should cause him worry:

If Tobias was late, the buyer would have to hold the freight cars; the expense would go up; the price for hogs would go down. That just couldn't happen. Tobias would work like a house afire to get there on time. He wouldn't allow the storm to come between him and three and a half cents.

Joss grinned in his sleep, flopped over, and slept easier for the rest of the night.

Chapter 15

Needed:
Water, Rest, and a Map

"Got any idea how far to water?"

"Whadja say, Joss?" Hank sat up in his blanket and gouged at his eyes.

"How far to water?"

"Oh, water. Yeah, I got some notion. Ain't we got any at all?"

"Just two part-full canteens. Not enough even for the horses. We got to find water before it gets hot. Top's doing first-rate bringing the hogs back. Got about a third in already. I 'spect they'll need water real soon, too."

Joss scanned the surrounding mountains that were now visible, rising way above their heads. "That landmark we picked was a real dud. It's behind them first mountains yonder, probably. We came downhill more'n I reckoned yesterday."

Hank was wide awake now, Sterling also. They stood and shook their blankets.

Joss turned away and went out to count the hogs that Firetop had collected. He counted thirty-eight.

"Good dog," Joss praised, rubbing the collie's ears.

Firetop slapped a wet lick on Joss's wrist and loped out the way he had come, only more to the left.

He's covering the area like it was a pie, Joss thought, wedging out from the center in all directions, which of course would be the only way to get the job done.

By mid-morning Firetop had brought in all but eight of the hogs.

"Get some meat in your belly, Top," Joss said, "then go find the rest. Here, you rate some water, too. We're moving now, got to. You can bring the hogs in wherever we are."

The horses were given a drink of water and a handful of oats.

Joss took his turn at the wagon.

When the sun shone directly down upon them, Firetop was in for the last time, and Joss knew from his satisfied actions—prancing up beside the wagon now and again—that all the hogs were now moving in the herd at the rear.

177

But still they had not found water.

Should they quit for rest time? Joss asked himself, or keep on? Which was most needed, rest or water? The air was warm, but it didn't seem as warm as yesterday at this time, before the storm. He decided to chance going on. Water, he knew, would be more important to man. With hogs, both were important.

They moved along easy, hour after hour, always going down, always edging a little to the right.

Night closed in and it was cool. They had not stopped to eat since their leaving in midmorning. Joss was afraid to stop, and the other boys, realizing his fear, said nothing. At least for a while.

When Hank saw, with the coming darkness, that Joss intended going on without a stop, he came up to the wagon.

"You losing your head, Joss?" he asked. "Them hogs is ready to wilt. You got to rest 'em some, even if just a hour, maybe. You'll have 'em all down with broken backs."

Joss kept the reins slack in his hands, but not so slack as to tell the horses they could stop. After a while he answered Hank.

"They got to have water, too. Which is worse—if they don't get up from broken backs, or because they're dead of thirst? We'll get on for a spell."

Hank swung on his heel and disappeared. Joss couldn't

tell if he left mad, but it didn't matter. What mattered now was to get over the next hump, to see if the moonlight disclosed a clump of willows that would suggest a spring or creek. If it didn't, like it didn't all afternoon, then you got yourself on, on over the next hump, as easy and careful as you could.

The moon was almost overhead when Joss noticed something peculiar happening alongside the slow-moving wagon. Instead of the hogs lagging behind, instead of his hearing from Hank or Sterling that hogs were bogging down now, that they would have to stop, the hogs were up with him!

For a while the vanguard of the herd kept pace with the wagon, and then, to Joss's further bewilderment, they were pulling ahead of him. They were excited and grunting and moving forward on seemingly strong and tireless legs.

And then Joss knew. He knew and he laughed to himself. The hogs smelled water!

Within moments the herd was gone, as the night before, bounding out into the darkness. Only now it was for a different reason.

Hank and Sterling walked with the team, sighing their relief, wondering how far hogs could smell water, or sense it.

Then a new problem entered Joss's mind. What if the water the hogs were heading for was the Clearwater

River? And if it was, and they rushed in too deep, or drank too much, or got chilled—

Joss stopped the team.

"Loose the horses, fellers, then follow me!" he yelped, and took out after the departed herd.

He flew up and down the moonswept humps of sage for what seemed like miles. He was glad that Firetop had gone with the herd.

And then he saw them, off to the west, lined up in a smudgy file.

It was a creek, not the river.

Joss reached the creek and found it to be a wide and shallow bed. He waded in and cupped a handful of water to his dry and dusty mouth. Was there anything better in all the world than a handful of water?

He proceeded down the creek, checking for deep holes and floundering animals. Firetop, too, was wading and watching and lapping at the water.

"We better get 'em back now, Top."

The hogs moved back under the collie's imperative barks.

Sterling, Hank, and the horses arrived at the creek at the same time. Joss took the horses, when they had drunk at the creek, and went back for the wagon. He felt good, now. The day's ending was just right.

They had not been driving too long the following day

when they came in view of the Clearwater River. It was about a mile distant, a whitish silver slice into the floor of the valley.

When they were yet a hundred yards away, with the sound of the river's torrent and might filling their ears, Joss said, "Hold 'em now, Top. We're going to stop for a look-see."

Joss reached the bank and stared the river full in the face, and could not help gasping just a little. The width of it, the power of its deep and rolling current, took his breath away. They couldn't cross it here, it was plain to see.

"Where do you reckon Houston come up to this, Hank?"

Hank was slow to answer. He was scanning the hills that rose over there across the river. He gazed down the river as far as he could see, until it became lost to view in a wide and bending sweep. Then his eyes turned upstream, and he found there the same pouring might of foamy clear water. He struggled to place this picture with the one in his mind of crossing the river with Houston. It didn't fit at all.

"Houston must have crossed downstream, Joss," Hank said at last. "If he crossed upriver, it can't be far up. We better check that first. If we don't see no fording place within a mile or so, we'll know it's got to be downstream. It was a dandy place to go over. I remember Houston

181

saying that it was even better than the regular one."

Sterling said, "I'll stay with Top and the herd. No use all three of us going. I'll get a fire going and some coals ready for dinner."

"Okay," Joss answered. "Let's go, Hank."

An hour later Sterling dished up baked potatoes and broiled venison steak. The boys consumed the meal with silent relish, topped it off with apples and two dried prunes apiece.

"You're a first-rate cook, Sterl," Joss said, and was seconded by Hank.

Joss said they might as well drive the hogs downriver now. The crossing had to be that way. Sterling suggested that he handle the wagon, leaving Joss and Hank free to confer and scout the crossing.

Several miles downriver, as they swung around a wide bend, Hank stopped and said this was the place.

Joss studied the current, the width of the flowing river. "It don't look like no crossing to me," he said. "Just looks like more of what we've been passing all day."

" 'Tis though, boss," Hank said. "Lookit!"

He gestured to the other side of the valley floor, across the river, where the humpy hillocks began once more. There, quite unmistakably, was a wide trail, winding from the rocky beach up into the humps. It was a broad and beaten path—though not recently used—one that numberless herds of hogs could have made.

182

Joss saw all this and knew that Hank had found his crossing, but his eyes, returning to the rolling current, foam-white in places, glass-clear and surging in others, told him that Hank was wrong.

"We can't cross here, though, Hank."

"I can see that, but it wasn't like this two years ago. Not nothing. It was smooth and shallow and wide. The hogs could have walked across, almost, but they didn't. They like to swim."

"I 'spect high water changed it," Joss said. "I heard Pop say something like that once. High water scoops out the river bottom sometimes, or a sand bar, and moves it downstream some place. Let's go on down a ways and see what it's like."

A half mile farther down they found what they were looking for, though not quite what they had hoped for. There was a wide bar of sand on the opposite side, protruding out into the water for fifty yards. But between it and their shore was a current gushing as though it was thrust through a funnel.

"If that's the sand from above," Joss remarked grimly, "we can't use it."

He signaled Sterling to stop there and wait. He and Hank proceeded on downriver.

In the hour or so of daylight remaining, they found nothing, absolutely nothing, no suitable place to cross the river. They turned back, weary and disheartened.

Did this mean that they would have to go clear back upstream to the regular crossing? That might take two days or even more. They couldn't spare two days—not now, not after the lightning storm. Still, they couldn't swim the hogs over anything they had seen so far. That was asking for no hogs in a hurry.

Maybe.

Joss's mind skipped to a new line of thought. There were bound to be some places that would be better to cross than others. Maybe not so good as he would want, or choose, but maybe good enough, if they worked it easy and right. He'd have to study the river closer, as soon as it got light in the morning—

With the dawn of the next day Joss was again on the bank of the river, walking it for a mile, then turning and walking back. He did this both up and down the river, with his new idea ever before his eyes.

Finally, he reached a decision. They would cross above the sand bar two hundred yards, just before the place where the river sliced in to make its headlong dive through the narrow channel. The more he studied this spot, the more Joss became convinced that it was the best one he had found. He stood now, considering it further.

For one thing, it was wide, and that meant, probably, that it wasn't as deep there, or the current as strong. It looked mighty wicked, even so, but there would likely

184

be no undertows, like he'd heard Pop talk of. Then there was the curve over there on the other side, where the water swept in to get by the sand bar. There was no current over there. That meant that if they could start fast and go steady they'd fight through the current and into quiet water before it pulled them into the trough. There would be plenty of time to cross. All they had to remember was to go easy and steady.

Joss squinted at the bright, new, rising sun. They'd have to get a move on. He hoped somebody had breakfast ready.

Chapter 16

Wrong River Crossing

"First thing is to test it," Joss stated. He had climbed a rock that overhung the river. He sat down on it now and began to unlace his boots.

"How, Joss?" Sterling stood close by, staring at Joss's chosen crossing.

The hogs were feeding on spilled wheat and corn. Joss wanted them full of food, but not too full. He wanted them in the water before their bodies got too warm under the glare of the rising sun.

"I'll swim it myself, first," Joss answered. "Somebody could be finding logs to float under the wagon. Only one thing we got to keep remembering. We go like holysmoke at first, then steady and easy. I'll tell you more when I get back."

186

Hank was unlacing his boots. "You'll be needing company," he said.

"I will no such thing, Hank Ames," Joss retorted. "Get 'em fastened back up. I want no charley horse to mess with out there. You can ride Sugar across. Sterl can take Old Priss."

"You hadn't ought to go it alone, though," Hank persisted.

Joss snickered. "What do I need somebody for? You couldn't help me if I did get swallered up. Besides, you need to be getting things ready to move when I get back."

He twisted out of his shirt and laid it carefully on the rock, alongside his boots and socks. He pulled off his pants and piled them on top of his shirt.

"S'long, fellers," he said, and bounded out into the river in a long shallow dive.

Sterling and Hank watched as Joss surfaced, cutting the water in long, swift strokes.

Joss didn't look back. His arms flashed up with the steadiness of waterwheel paddles, bringing him ever closer to the strongest current in mid-river. His feet churned a small fountain in his wake.

"He's in it, now," Hank muttered tensely.

Sterling didn't want to look, but he did. He made himself look. He didn't know how he was ever going to cross, even on horseback. But he'd have to. This was not something he could quit just because he realized he wasn't

187

good at it, like baseball, or fighting, or making friends.

And so Sterling forced himself to look, to watch Joss's head bobbing in the current, to watch the current pull him downstream as if he were a rubber ball. His heart thumped loud in his mouth and ears and every place in his body, and still he looked.

Firetop crouched on the bank, unnoticed by the two staring boys. For a moment, as his eyes followed Joss moving out across the water, his body poised, as if to lunge in after him. Then, abruptly, he changed positions, sitting tautly on his haunches, his ears pointed sharply, and watched.

"He's gaining on it!" Hank sang out. "See there! He's across the worst of it!"

Sterling nodded silently. He had seen, too, though he could hardly believe it. But there was Joss, now beyond the stronger currents, his arms still beating an up-and-down pattern.

When he reached the quiet, protected water of the inner sandbank, Joss flipped over onto his back.

"That's right," Hank said, "get over and rest. That was topnotch. I sure admire his way with the water, Sterl."

Sterling nodded. He couldn't answer. He told himself to quit shaking. It was all over.

"I guess we can hunt for them logs, now, Sterl."

188

They were dragging a log down to the river when Joss made a rush into the water, from far upstream, and began the swim back.

It seemed to Sterling that he had only breathed a half a dozen times from the time Joss began his churn across till he was there, climbing out fifty feet above the rock that held his clothes.

"We got river to spare," he told Sterling and Hank, "if everything goes right. Notice where I kicked over?" He meant where he had left the current on the first crossing and struck quiet water.

"It don't look like trouble," Hank said. "What spooks me some, though, is the wagon. It'll be slow getting across the current."

"I know it." Joss's brow was furrowed as he pulled on his pants. "If we didn't need it so bad, I'd say chuck it, get it on the way back. But we got to have the feed, enough for two more days. The horses can't pack that much. And our grub box, too. I was thinking maybe I could rope it to Sug's harness and have you ready to cut it if it looked like it wasn't going to make it across in time. I think it will, though."

"Sounds like it would, probably," Hank agreed.

Sterling offered to stay with the wagon on the crossing, but Joss would have none of that.

"Too risky, Sterl. If we had to cut the rope you'd be

a goner. Nope. Old Priss is strong. She'll get you across."

"We got one log for the float," Hank said. "We better hunt up another one, Sterl."

It proved to be more of a job putting a raft under the wagon than the boys anticipated. But finally the logs were forced into position and lashed in place with ropes.

"Now, Hank," Joss said, "get Sugar out in front of the wagon."

Hank mounted Sugar and led her down into the water.

Sterling fastened an inch manilla-hard rope to the wagon tongue—a rope on each side—and brought these up to fasten on both sides of Sugar's harness, so that the pull of the wagon would be balanced. About twenty-five feet of rope separated the wagon tongue from the tail of the horse.

Hank was prepared to go, his knife in readiness in a sheath at his side.

Sterling and Joss got behind the wagon, where the raft logs protruded, ready to shove.

Firetop had the hogs close to the water. He awaited a signal from Joss to start them in.

Everything was in readiness.

Joss glanced out across the river to their destination. It looked longer, across, than it really was. He glanced around him, making sure of the collie, sure of Old Priss, standing off to one side. He tried to ignore an uneasy tingle that was climbing his spine, now that the moment of action had come. Everything depended on the success of the crossing, even their lives.

He shouted, "Let's go!" before the feeling got too deep inside him.

He and Sterling heaved on the logs, which were now partially buried in shoreline mire.

Hank yelled, "Come on, Sug!" He spanked his mount urgently on the rump.

Sugar rolled an eye sideways and pulled.

Joss felt the logs break free and watched as they bobbed to the surface, the wagon atop them wobbling as if in a windstorm.

In only seconds they were yards from shore, the wagon settling a little on its float. Hank was down over Sugar's ears, urging her to move faster.

"Okay, Sterl, hop on Old Priss and take right out. Leave her have her head. She'll know to get right along."

Sterling rushed to Old Priss. He knew he would have to get to her fast, mount and get out there where there would be no turning back. He felt dizzy and sick. He had to concentrate hard on keeping his balance as he swung into the saddle. He just could not fall on his face here, when everything depended on a quick start.

It seemed like years before Sterling felt the saddle snug up to him. He grasped out for the reins. He couldn't see a thing. He found them at last.

"Go, Old Priss!" he gasped out. "Go quickly!"

Old Priss stepped down into the water with utmost calm. She lunged out into deep water in a big splash and commenced to swim with strong, powerful pulls of her legs.

As Old Priss hit the water, Joss called, "Come, pig pig! Come, pig pig pig! Okay, Top, get 'em in here! Get 'em in here fast!"

Already they were hunched together on the bank. Now, without hesitation, they took to the water. They bobbed on the surface like corks. They were all in the water and swimming in a matter of seconds.

Joss glanced out to where Hank led with Sugar. He had almost reached the beginning of the mid-river current. They had slipped downriver quite a ways, Joss thought, but not too far. They still had room to slip more. And they'd need it. His eyes came back to Old Priss. He couldn't tell, from the way Sterling sat the saddle, how he was faring, but he must be okay. He was sitting tight.

"Okay, Top, we'd better light out. All you got to do is swim, dog."

Firetop sprang into the water a fraction of a second after Joss's dive and struck out with confident strokes.

And so, being in the water, stroking easy and low over the river's surface, Joss missed the catastrophe beginning to take place up ahead.

Sugar had plunged into the mid-river current at the

top of her swimming speed and was instantly swept downstream.

"It's okay, Sug horse," Hank assured. "We're doing topnotch. Just keep on like you been doing. We'll make 'er through."

If anything, the horse had not decreased her exertion, but increased it as she felt the current sweep her down. She had almost crossed the worst of the surging water when the raft came into it, full force.

For a second or so the going was easy. There was no pull on Sugar whatsoever, for the current was lashing the raft downriver in a swift and wrenching thrust. The rope that connected the wagon to Sugar became whipped and slack in the glass-clear water. The wagon plunged down the current, freesailing, for though it was still connected to Sugar's harness, the leverage was gone. There was nothing to break its speed. Nothing until it passed Sugar, till it once again, on the downriver side, came to the end of its tether.

Then, in one gigantic, cracking jerk, the front of the raft shot around, facing upstream, and the rope whipped tight once more.

Hank had seen, seconds before, what was going to happen. He knew he had only seconds to break out of the mid-river current, or he would be caught with a double load—the helpless wagon on a downstream pull, and the battle just he and Sugar were engaged in, getting over the worst of the current.

"Go, Sug, go!" Hank cried sharply.

Sugar was pressing along at the top of her power already. She could go no faster.

They wouldn't make it.

Hank saw that they wouldn't make it. He had only partially braced himself for the jolt he knew was coming, when it hit.

One of his hands was twisted in around Sugar's mane. It was that hold that kept him from being tossed over into the current.

The horse was flicked about like a piece of driftwood, back into a trough of current, and swept downstream, pulled by the surge of the water and the rope attached to her harness. One portion of the pull-rope, on the right side, was slung against Hank, pushing and pulling against him, almost whipping him out of the saddle.

Hank struggled against the rope. It felt like it was slicing through his ribs. He fought to slip under it, to allow it to cross over him so that he could straighten up. It was necessary that he straighten up. Not only would he be thrashed out of the saddle and into the current unless he could free himself immediately, but also, this way, he could not possibly reach his scabbard. This meant that he could not save Sugar.

His right arm, the one closest to the scabbard, was pinioned against his waist by the pressure of the rope. His left hand could not reach the knife by a thread's margin. His fingers, straining and stretching, only tickled the scabbard's edges.

Hank fought, heaving on the rope with all the desperate strength of his fourteen years. Away. He had to push the rope away. He realized, even as he fought, that he was waging a futile battle, and so was Sugar. She, just as desperately as her rider, was struggling to regain the momentum of her giant, plowing strokes. But shock was still in her from the awful jolt. Her legs moved weakly.

If Hank yielded to the force of the rope and allowed it to topple him into the river, he would still have to fight the current, and fight to get on the other side of Sugar. And Sugar would be the helpless victim of the river and the raft, pulling her relentlessly downstream.

Hank twisted his neck for a glance downriver, to see, if he could, how close they were to the trough. What he saw was a picture that would live long and brilliantly in his memory.

Sterling was sitting high and straight on Old Priss. He was riding the horse, not across, but *into the down current!* They were working with the current, slipping fast downstream.

The glimpse Hank received of Sterling's face, as he

swept by, was one of deep concentration of purpose.

Sterling's hand flashed up, and in it shone a knife blade. It reached out and down and severed the ropes that stretched tight into the water before him, that still connected Sugar to the raft.

Hank braced his legs. He was free!

"Now we can go, Sug!" he yelled joyously to the horse. "We'll make 'er through, now!"

Almost instantly Hank felt the animal's reaction to freedom from the rope. Her legs bit strongly into the current, found brace, pushed, and bit again.

They were gaining! Hank felt relief wash into him. He swung for a look downriver, where Sterling would be pushing out of the strong current also. The wagon was lost, but—

196

What the—? Hank struggled to correct his vision by staring hard, but he still saw the same thing:

Sterling hadn't turned! He was still going downriver. And now—what was this?

A rope was twirling down there, out over Sterling's head. It was spinning in a thin silver ring. It was the riata, the one Ropejon had given Sterling. The noose was big, as big as a house, it looked like.

Sugar was out of the strong current now and heading across the semi-rough water for the inlet. Hank was no help, not even offering verbal encouragement. His attention was glued to Sterling and his beautiful riata. He was so transfixed by what he saw that he could not even yell at Sterling to quit his tomfooling and get across the current, that he didn't have much river left before it began its powerful sweep into the trough.

The riata snaked out across the air. The tip of the noose seemed to pause for a split second, resting and lilting, before dipping and diving toward the water. It dropped quickly then, the point of the loop disappearing as the ring became wider. It fell square and sure on top of the rafted wagon. The forepart of the loop settled round the posts that formed the wagon rack. The hind part of the loop fell into the current in front of the wagon tongue. Sterling then gave the riata a peculiar twist and jerk, the curl of it instantly sweeping the length of the rope, to end where the loop floated atop the wagon tongue. The curl popped the riata out from its slack position and flipped it under the wagon tongue.

He had a sure hold on it, now, under the tongue and around the posts. He wrapped his end of the riata around Old Priss's chest.

Old Priss had already faced cross-current, her legs plowing the water's surge.

Joss had gained quiet water and was staring in profound bewilderment downriver, when Sterling, towing the wagon, rode out of mid-current into the weaker force

198

beyond. Hank was already across on Sugar, wading out, down from him fifty yards. Old Priss would make it, too, Joss could see, only by a much closer margin than Sugar.

Not only was Joss bewildered, he was helpless to help. He rolled back on his stomach and swam for shore.

The hogs were climbing out, now, all up and down the bank. They had accomplished the crossing as if they enjoyed it.

Joss found bottom and gushed through the water to shore and then downriver.

Sterling and Old Priss had reached quiet water and were trailing in slow, pulling the wagon after them.

Joss reached Hank first. "Nab it!" he cried. "What happened out there?"

"It—it—" The words wouldn't come out of Hank. He was in the throes of reaction.

"It was awful," he managed finally. "Sterl did it all. It was awful."

"Yeah?" Joss said. He had never seen Hank so wrought up. "Well, take 'er easy, now."

He left Hank on the run, heading down the bank to where Sterling would come in.

"Toss the riata here, Sterl!" Joss called. "I'll hold while you get out!"

"All right," Sterling answered. He unwound the rope from Old Priss and tossed it to Joss.

When he had dismounted, Sterling turned to look up-river. "The hogs are in, I see," he said. "They all must have made it across all right."

"Sterl, you son-of-a-gun, what happened out there? Hank's so tuckered he can't even talk."

Sterling's gaze flitted hurriedly across the river that he had just climbed out of.

"I don't want to either, Joss," he said, his voice hardly above a whisper. "After a while, when it isn't so new, I'll tell you. Shall we start unlashing the raft?"

"Yeah," Joss said, understanding, at least in part. "We'll do that first off."

Later that day, when the hogs were feeding, and after the boys had eaten a scanty meal and were resting by the fire, Hank told Joss the story.

"What made you do it, Sterl?" Joss asked, marveling at his cousin's courage, though feeling that he still didn't understand it. He omitted the rest of what he was think-ing: How come you to do it when most times you're such a puny sissy, sort of?

"What made me?" Sterling asked uncertainly. "Why, you know why, Joss. We have to get the hogs to Prairie Town. We needed the feed—"

"Yeah, yeah," Joss cut in. He felt like hugging Sterling and bawling, telling him he was okay, even though he still didn't understand what made Sterling do it, not really. He wanted to hug Hank, too, and tell him he was okay. But he didn't.

Instead, he stood up and stuffed his hands into his pockets and glared at the fire.

Then he said, "We better hit the hay. We got the bluff to climb tomorrow."

Hank and Sterling came to their feet and went with Joss to get their blankets.

Chapter 17

The Pay-off

Though Joss felt certain that the hogs were traveling first-rate, hardly losing any weight on the drive so far, he was nonetheless vigilant on the climb to the prairie.

He and Hank walked the herd constantly, studying this hog and then that one, watching for signs of fatigue, of spine weakening, of diarrhea, sunstroke, and loss of appetite. None of these ailments had yet appeared, but this was no proof that some of them would not, in the time and distance remaining.

Rests were called frequently on the climb up Houston's grade. The drive road wasn't too steep for hogs, but the hogs didn't like it, and complained in angry snorts and grunts. Joss humored them with twice as many rests as he thought they actually needed. He humored them because he didn't know, really, if their protests were just ordinary hog dislike of climbing, or if this might spell a first symptom of some ailment, or of total exhaustion.

Springs were well marked on the grade. It seemed to Joss that Houston, too, had called many rest and watering stops on the upward climb.

The herd broke over the top of the gorge on the evening of the second day since leaving the Clearwater. The horizon, out to the west and north, was streaked with the last brilliant swaths of a setting sun.

Joss came up over the top and stopped. There was the landmark peak! It appeared to be just as far away now as it did when they first spotted it and called it their own. It beat all how distance could fool you in this air. The peak would be way past Prairie Town.

Tonight would be their last night on the trail. What would tomorrow bring? Would the going price be two and a half cents or three? It would have to be at least two and a half—And Tobias—he'd have to reach Prairie Town about the same time Tobias got there—

Joss signaled to Sterling to go ahead with the wagon. Several miles in from the rim, they found another of Houston's marked springs and called a halt.

While dinner was cooking—some shriveled carrots and parsnips and a venison roast—the boys decided that laundry time had arrived. They skinned off their pants and shirts and took turns scrubbing them in the water pail, with cold water and the camp's one bar of soap. It hadn't diminished, to speak of, since Joss's mother had handed it to him the night before the start.

After the meal Joss disposed of the deer carcass, salvaging the best of the hams.

After the meal it was decided that they, themselves, could do with some scrubbing. Again, turns were taken at the pail and soap.

"You'll have to dig in harder'n that, Hank," Joss counseled, "else you'll still look like a halfbreed when we hit town. You got soot clean up into your hair."

"Just 'cause you crossed the river sixteen times," Hank retorted, "and got your black soaked off, no need for you to mama me."

"Up to you," Joss flung back. "Just figured you'd want to look slick for them gals you been dreaming about."

"On second consideration, Mister Melborne," Hank said gravely, "you can be my looking glass. I know a pretty little daisy in that town that's probably been crying her eyes out, waiting for me to come back."

They badgered each other in this manner until they were clean and presentable to each other's satisfaction. Since it was very dark by then, with only the campfire for light, they decided to wait till morning to straighten up the wagon for their town visit.

Everyone was awake before dawn and anxious to be gone on this last lap of the drive. Their clothes, hung on willow switches close to the fire, were almost dry. They put them on damp and in no time had forgotten about their cold wetness.

The day was cloudless and clear and blue, if you looked up. If you looked down, the day was brown and golden, the brown of cheat and bunch grass with the sheen of the sun upon it.

They came into the main road before noon. Prairie Town could be seen in the distance, only a mile or so away.

Joss studied the road before him. Hogs had passed over this area only hours before. There had been a lot of them; they had covered a full acre of driving width.

It was Tobias! Joss said to himself, his heart beating faster. It would almost have to be!

He wanted to yell to Sterling to step up the pace of the wagon; to order Firetop to run the hogs. But he did neither one. He circled the herd in his usual manner, trying to keep his mind on watching for flaws, even though he realized that he was bringing to Prairie Town a herd of hogs in perfect condition. The buyer would see this, Joss was sure.

"I never did see time mope along so, did you, boss?" Hank was bypassing Joss on his rounds in and through and around the hogs. He slashed a shirt sleeve across his wet forehead. "Seems like we been coming into town for twenty hours."

It was afternoon, now. The boys had not stopped to eat. Joss could think of nothing but reaching the hog corrals and the buyer before the buyer got through with Tobias and left.

Joss went ahead, now, with Hank. Sterling would follow in more slowly, leading the herd that Firetop was keeping in shape.

The two boys circled the town and came to the hog corrals. They passed several empty ones before coming to the bunches of men standing in front of several very bulging pens of snorting and grunting hogs.

Joss spotted Tobias talking to a huge, red-faced man.

"That's Red," Hank whispered in Joss's ear. "He's the buyer that was here last year, too. He don't put up with Tobias's noise very long."

"What?" Joss mumbled. "Tobias trying to raise the price?"

"What else? Red listens just so long, then walks away and leaves Tobias talking to himself."

The boys paused several paces away, prepared to wait until Red walked away from Tobias.

Tobias spotted Joss and stopped talking, leaving his mouth hanging open.

"There he is!" Tobias shrilled now, a soiled and skinny finger pointing at Joss. "There's my other seventy hogs! That will make the seven hundred I bargained for! I got your word on three and a half! You can't go back on your say so!'' Tobias's voice had mounted rapidly to a thin, high register, cutting through the air like a sharp, quick whip. "I'll have my three and a half! I demand it!"

The fleshy, red-faced buyer glanced down with growing impatience on the raging man before him.

"You still don't get it through your head, do you, Tobias?'' Red said.

It was plain to all the men and boys that had grouped close after Tobias's outburst, that Red was struggling to keep his temper.

"I told you twice already,'' Red said, "and I'll tell you once more. The bottom fell out of hogs two days back. Everybody is loaded with hogs. The slaughterhouses are loaded with hogs. We're swimming in hogs. We don't know what to do with them, we got so many. Try to get that through your head, Tobias. I don't want your hogs. I don't know what I'll do with them after I get them. I only came up with the cars because I said I'd come. Now, one more last time, I'll take the hogs, the whole stinking, foul, robbing mess of them, for two cents a pound, even the boy's hogs, yonder, that just came in. Where you got your hogs, son?''

It was useless for Joss to try to speak. He heard Red's question and realized that he was being spoken to, but he couldn't open his mouth.

He felt like he was in a frozen mold, like the time when

Toppy attacked the wild sow. He could move nothing about him. His breathing was light, almost nil. He was in a frozen bubble marked *Two Cents*. It wrapped him tight in its icy bands of shock.

Not only did he feel this frozen mold encasing him, he did not want to break it away. He did not wish to stand out from it and face the awful, horrible, terrible truth.

The crowd was staring at the boys now, waiting for one of them to speak.

Hank answered, after he, too, had stared at Joss.

"They're out a ways, Red," he said. "Where do you want 'em?"

"Right here, sonny." Red indicated an empty corral on his left. "Get them in here as quick as you can. I aim to load up and be out of here by dark."

"Come on, Joss," Hank muttered, punching Joss's ribs. "Kick out of it."

"No," Joss heard himself saying, as if from a great distance.

He was walking toward Red. He was walking stiff and straight.

"I can't take two cents, Red," he said. "I can take two and a half. Two and a half would do it. My Pop's got to walk, see, and he hasn't got much time for this operation. He's got to have it right away. Two and a half would do it right well."

Except for the noise the hogs were making, the runway

between the corrals was dead quiet. The men and boys were trying to make sense out of Joss's words. They could see that the boy spoke with difficulty. His words came out stiff and stilted, like his walk.

Hank came up beside Joss.

"What he means, Red," Hank clarified, "is that his Pop got hurt and needs an operation to walk again. He drove these hogs over a hundred miles to sell 'em so his Pop could have the operation, see. The operation costs five hundred dollars. Joss don't mean nothing disrespectful, ya understand. He ain't quite himself, is all. Let down, kind of."

Red was looking at Joss. He didn't need any more explanation. His big lips drew together. He held them together thoughtfully.

"Joss," he said at last, "I'd give you more if I could. I don't set the price. I just work for an outfit that does. Now, I've never said this before in my life, but I'll say it to you, now. I'm sorry the price dropped two days ago. For you, I'm really sorry."

"Let's go, Joss," Hank urged, a hand poking at Joss's waist.

It took several steps for Joss to get turned around. He stalked out of the runway like he was a piece of wooden fence.

Red watched Joss's stilted and icy retreat and knew that the boy was close to heartbreak.

"I wish there was something I could do, Joss," Red called. "Sure be glad to help if I could."

It was Hank who glanced back and said, "Much oblige anyway, Red."

An hour later, when Red handed to Joss currency and coin in the amount of three hundred and eighty dollars, Joss took it and moved away.

He didn't walk so fence-post straight, now, but neither did he move as Joss Melborne was accustomed to moving. Only one aspect of his carriage had not changed, either when he heard the stunning news, or now, when he walked away from the buyer one hundred and twenty dollars short of the needed amount. His shoulders still hung straight across his body. They did not droop in defeat.

As a matter of fact, defeat had not occurred to Joss, not as a concrete and final fact.

He paused, now, stepping into an empty passageway that dipped through the sides of the corrals. Hank and Firetop followed.

Joss put the money away. He had brought a belt along expressly for this purpose, one that had inside pockets. He put the money in carefully and drew it around his waist once more.

"You're not heading back tonight, are ya, Joss?" Hank asked. He had long ago accepted the fact that there would be no forthcoming oyster dinner. Or boots. That was

210

okay. All he asked, now, was to wait for the dance. This was Saturday.

"We could light out first thing in the morning, couldn't we, Joss?"

"I don't plan on going yet," Joss said.

"That so?" Hank asked, astonished.

"That's so." They were out of the passageway, now. Joss stopped again, facing Hank.

"I got to get to thinking," he said, "by myself."

"That so?" Hank asked, feeling stupid. Then he realized that Joss was telling him to leave him alone.

"Okay, Joss, sure," Hank said, and for some reason felt uneasy. "Meet ya at the wagon after while?"

Joss nodded without speaking. He left Hank staring after him.

Hank watched as Joss turned out into the open prairie, Firetop close at his side.

"Now what the Sam Hill?" Hank asked himself. He stared after Joss for several minutes, watching as he walked along in his kind of lost but upright fashion. Then Hank turned and moved in the direction of the wagon and Sterling.

Sterling had stayed to watch the wagon and horses when the hogs were being driven into the pens.

Hank wanted to talk to Sterling about Joss. Somehow, he had lost interest in the dance.

Chapter 18

A Last-ditch Resort

In less than an hour Joss was turning his footsteps toward the wagon.

He came from the direction of the main street. He was walking somewhat hurriedly, yet his steps were small. The reason for this was that something big was stirring in his mind. Something big—and daring.

It had not taken complete shape yet. It was like a big, exciting shadow that had not yet loomed bright into the sunlight of his thoughts. And so he walked quickly, eagerly, but his steps were short. He was struggling to push the shadowy idea into the light of day.

This vague and exciting idea had entered his mind while he was listening to the talk of a cluster of men in front of one of the saloons. He had wandered onto the main street minutes before, from the open prairie. He had gleaned nothing from his thinking out there, except confirmation of his prior conviction that, somehow, he had to get more money.

The men lounging in front of the saloon had been like any ranchers and farmers that Joss knew about. What had caught his attention, as he wandered by, was what one of them said:

"Not when we had them turtle races, by grab, it warn't dull!"

Joss was attracted by this remark. He had never heard of such an outlandish notion as a turtle race. He paused close by the group and listened. No one noticed him. The conversation continued.

"I reckon the whole country's dyin' down," someone else said. "Not just hog prices. I haven't seen anything different or sensayshnull since them turtle races back in eighty-one."

"That was years ago," a young man put in. "I remember about them races, just barely. They was started by some minstrel wandering through the country. I sure remember how everybody took bets on the turtles, though, on which ones they figured to win. I remember how riled up and excited everybody got. Seems kind of silly, now, getting so fussed up and betting money on turtles."

"It was different, that's why," an elderly man retorted almost indignantly. "People hanker for somethin' different." Then he added with an owlish look, "But bein' different takes brains. That's what that minstrel was, brainy."

Joss stared at the men, and at what they said.

"Sure is dull, now," another remarked with a sigh. "Just Saturday night shindigs get tiresome."

Joss turned away, leaving them quickly. He wanted to be alone with the shadowy idea that these men's words had caused.

They want something exciting, his thoughts were saying. They would bet money on something that would cause them excitement and fun.

Then there came to Joss's mind the incident last summer at the swimming hole, how Hank had made fun of Sterling's attempts to lasso a hog and said, "Just whistle when the show's on. I'll take bets on the hog."

And then, like a light switched on, the shadow was a shadow no longer, but an idea, full-blown, standing clear and brilliant in his mind.

He stopped still in his tracks, his eyes wide open, seeing the picture his mind had painted.

When his legs started moving again toward the wagon, they were going fast. In a half a dozen steps he was running, running as fast as his legs would travel.

He burst in upon Sterling and Hank, bolting to a stop only inches short of crashing into them. They were seated round a small fire, looking disconsolate and blue.

"You look plumb hog wild, Joss," Hank remarked, coming to his feet. "You rob a bank or something?"

214

"Nope," Joss gasped. He stood before them, legs spread, breathing hard, glancing from Sterling to Hank and back again.

"Or maybe I am hog wild, Hank," he said. "Maybe I am. But Pop said you got to be hog wild sometimes."

Joss's eyes were resting on his cousin.

"Sterl," he said, taking a deep breath, "I got to ask you something. I got a idea on how to make the rest of that five hundred. But it isn't no good without you. Without you it won't work at all. How'd you like to rope a hog for the city of Prairie Town?"

Sterling stared at Joss, his face completely baffled and blank.

"Well, well, of course, I suppose," he stammered. What did Joss mean? "But I don't quite see—"

"People here are plumb dying from lack of excitement, see, Sterl?" Joss broke in. "They even used to take bets on turtle races, just for something to do. Now a hog roping—nobody's ever seen a hog roping. In fact, everybody knows it can't be done. People have tried lots of times and been laughed at, like you, remember?"

Sterling nodded. He would never forget it; it would be his shameful, red flag reminder, in case he ever felt like showing off—

Quite suddenly Sterling's face lost the ruddiness it had acquired the last few months. He couldn't rope a hog, not like that— I'm not good at it—even—not really—

"Well," Joss was steaming on, "we'll stage a show for

215

'em. A hog roping show! We'll take bets, see? Maybe we can even get two-to-one bets against you! That'll bring our money up to five hundred dollars quick as scat!"

Hank asked, "You'd use your money in your belt to take bets, Joss?"

"You bet! I was thinking I might even ask Red if he'd have time to help. He could take charge of the bets and money and stuff. He said he'd help if he could."

"You mean to have it right away? Before dark?"

"Be the best, while so many folks are in town, and just before Red takes off."

"Jumpin' geecracks!" Hank yelped, warming to the idea. "We better get to spreading the word fast. We don't want to miss any ranchers that'll be heading home right away."

"What do you say, Sterl?" Joss asked. "Shall we do it?"

"I—I don't think I could do it," Sterling got out. "You know how I am."

"You bet I know how you are, Sterl," Joss shot back. "I know you're the best roper I ever did see. I know you roped a hog, one that was running. I know you roped a wagon that was barreling down the middle of the Clearwater like crazy. I wouldn't even a thought of this if I thought you couldn't do it."

"The wagon was different." Sterling's voice was a whisper. He wished his mouth wasn't so dry.

"How different?" Joss demanded.

"I—well—we needed the wagon—and I forgot about

216

being so—well—so—" He couldn't think of a word that fitted what he wanted to say.

"Kind of no-account, you mean, Sterl?" Joss was glaring at his cousin. He dismissed Hank's presence as presenting a handicap. There wasn't time, now, for secret talks.

"I—well—yes—I guess that's what I mean."

"You got the wagon out, though, Sterl." Hank joined the tense and crucial conversation. "You was risking your life then."

"What made you forget then, Sterl," Joss asked, "when you was getting the wagon out, about being so no-account?"

Sterling wished for the ground to swallow him up, or lightning to strike him dead, thus ending this torturous examining of his dark and unpleasant depths.

"Oh," he said, "well, we needed the feed, like I said—"

"Why did we need the feed?" Joss questioned, almost ruthlessly.

"Well, for the hogs, of course. They needed to arrive in good shape—"

"Why?" Joss said.

"Well, for the money—"

"What's the difference, then or now? We need the money just as bad now."

"And it ain't like you never roped a hog, Sterl," Hank put in. "You roped one good and stout. You got a riata, a thin one. I can see where roping a hog with a riata like that would work. The trick is, nobody else'll tumble. Nobody ever tried to rope a hog with a quarter-inch riata, probably."

The riata *does* make a difference. The thought pierced into Sterling's clogged and trembling brain. And I did rope a hog once. It would be for Uncle Morris, the same reason that we trailed the hogs all the way here, like Joss said—

"What if I fail?" Sterling heard himself asking. "Then you wouldn't have any money at all."

"We won't need any," Joss answered simply, "if we don't get five hundred. You know Pop."

"Yes, I know that," Sterling said. "I know that," he repeated, as if reminding himself that he knew. "And of course that is the thing to keep foremost in mind." Sterling drew air into his lungs in jerky spasms.

"All right, Joss. I'll try. I'll try my very best."

"You won't have to just try, Sterl," Joss said, feeling like shouting and turning cartwheels. "You'll give this town the biggest show since the turtle races!"

Sterling managed a weak smile. "I just hope it works," he said.

Minutes later Hank was off for the main street of Prairie Town to spread the news of a hog roping show. Joss headed for the hog corrals to see Red.

He found him standing outside a narrow chute leading from one of the pens up into a railroad car. His usually red face was purple. He was engaged in calling upon the gods and lightning and earthquakes to assist him in getting one stubborn, ornery hog to enter the freight car.

Joss, grinning, found a piece of two-by-six leaning against a fence. He picked it up and carried it inside the chute. He used the board as a shield until he had maneuvered behind the hog. Then he stove the board between the hog's hind legs and lifted. The hog snorted in futile protest and leaped into the car. It was a red Duroc, with Tobias's mark on its ear. Joss noticed something else, also. It was a sow. Tobias's mad sow. Joss felt belated fear as he stepped out of the chute. Tobias had found his lost sow after all. He wondered if he had hunted the sow himself. Probably. He would if no one else would.

Red mopped his face on a bedraggled handkerchief and reached into his pocket for his money pouch. "By grab, that's worth a dollar, sonny," he said, digging into the pouch. "I never saw that done before. Here you are. Well, Joss, isn't it?"

Joss nodded. "I'd as soon not take the money, Red. I came over to ask a favor."

"And did one," Red sighed. He noticed the change that had come over Joss. "Hope I can do it, son. Shoot."

Joss told him about his idea, about the men in front of the saloon, the turtle races, and Sterling and his skill with the riata and roping a hog.

Red listened attentively.

"You mean," Red said, when Joss had finished, "you mean this friend of yours can actually rope a hog?" He couldn't believe it. He had seen it tried, in his various dealings with hogs. He had never seen it accomplished.

"He can, okay, Red. Sterl's a first-rate roper."

Disbelief was still written on Red's face. "Well. And where do I come in?"

"We don't know nothing about taking bets and things, not for a big show. We thought if you had time you might—"

Joss got no further. He could see from the smile beginning on Red's face that he didn't need to say anything more.

"You die hard, don't you, son?" he said. "Sure, I'll handle the business end. Be glad to. It sounds right interesting. In fact, it's the first interesting thing about hogs I ever heard of."

Red fished his pocket watch out and studied it. "I got to rattle out of here inside of three hours. That gives us two hours to get ready and an hour for the show. Should be time enough."

"Plenty, Red!" Joss was beaming. "And much oblige. I figure to pay you for your trouble."

"Oh, no, Joss, the show will be payment enough. Them codgers was right. We do need some excitement. Now, let's see, first thing—"

Joss and Red got down to planning. They were deciding how to give out the tickets when Hank burst in on them.

220

"I got the whole town buzzing like a beehive!" Hank chortled. "Only now it's ready to pop wide open on account of what Tobias up and asked."

"Yeah?" Joss queried.

"You'd know, Joss, if you'd just turn your mind to it for ten seconds. The old skinflint is really painin' because of the drop on the price of hogs. He's plumb burning. You know what he had the downright nerve to ask me, Joss?" Hank was enjoying himself.

"Time's desertin' us fast," Joss retorted. "Let's have it."

"Yeah. Well, Tobias said, he said, 'You go tell that Joss Melborne that I'll bet with him. Tell him I'll bet all of my hog money for all of his if his cousin lassoes my ornery sow.' Can you beat that, Joss? And the town's plumb gone off its rockers. Everybody wants to know, is it going to be a wild hog roping show?"

"You can just trot back," Joss said, standing, his face tense with anger, "and tell Tobias and everybody else that we aren't staging this show for somebody to get killed."

Sterling was advancing toward them down the runway. He paused beside Hank. His expression was one of strained composure.

"They were asking me at the wagon, too," Sterling said. "I think it's a good idea. I told them I would do it."

Joss's face blanched white. He came in front of Sterling, his eyes furious. "You're not going to," he stated flatly,

221

his voice loaded with wrath. "We're not staging no murder show."

Sterling returned Joss's glare for a few moments in silence. Then he said, his voice calm, "I see no reason to get so flustered. A mad hog can't see any better than a sane one. Neither one can see what is above or beside it. I think I'll use a platform of some sort—"

Joss wasn't listening, now. He was mulling over, with amazement, the change in his cousin. He was no longer the wishywashy, follow-the-leader, fear-crazed person he had been an hour ago, and all summer and fall, with very few exceptions. He was afraid, still. Joss could see that he was afraid, even now. But it was different, sort of like he had lassoed his fear—

He considered Sterling's words. He knew Sterling was right about what a hog could see. A hog couldn't see above itself, at close range. If Sterl was to get a box of some kind, a good sturdy one, the hog couldn't see him. And the people could see Sterling better. Was there any danger for Sterling in this?

"We could make the platform heavy," Joss said, voicing his thoughts. "We'd have to keep Top out."

"We'd better have it in the end corral," Red advised. "It's open all around, with seats. Folks here call it the auction yard."

Joss and Sterling were eyeing each other. Then their hands were on each other's shoulders, gripping deep.

"Who's hog wild, now, I'd like to know?" Joss grumbled.

222

"I always was a good copycat," Sterling answered.

"Is it the auction yard, then, with the mad sow?" Red asked. "Time's skedaddlin' away, fellers."

"That's it," Sterling replied.

"All right," Red said decisively. "You taking Tobias's offer, Joss?"

"On a two-to-one," Joss answered promptly. "My three hundred doubled from Tobias, when Sterl wins. I'll leave him some to get home on."

"You tell that to Tobias, Hank," Red instructed. "If he goes for it, tell him to see me. Tell him he will also be responsible for getting the sow off the car and into the auction yard when it's time.

"Now Joss, you won't have money for bets if Tobias is on, so we'll just charge admission.

"Spread the word, Hank, after you get Tobias's okay on the bet. Grownups a dollar, children free. Seven o'clock sharp, in the auction yard. Now let's scatter. I'll help Hank. You boys get your platform ready. We got about an hour."

Sterling and Joss hooked up the team and moved the wagon alongside the auction yard. Then they went in search of boards and a hammer and nails.

Sterling wished that seven o'clock would hurry and arrive. He didn't know how long he could keep up this act he had started.

Chapter 19

Rope a Wild Hog

At ten minutes before seven there were no more empty seats in the Prairie Town auction yard. Families were packed onto benches so tightly that fathers were holding their smallest youngsters on their laps. There was much laughing and visiting and wonder over such an unheard-of event as a hog roping show, and a crazy hog at that.

"Even if he's good," one woman called to another, "I still don't see how it could be done. Sonny tried to get a hog out of my flower patch one day, and he's real good at roping cows. Well, all he managed to do was to tear up my flowers even worse. We never did get that hog out till it was good and ready to go!"

"I know!" the other woman answered. "George says the boy is bound to be good, to have them take on such a big bet—I heard they bet everything they got on their hogs. George says the show will be worth the money, all right enough. But to win! Why, George says it's utterly fantastic!"

A few bets were being wagered by the crowd. "Hey there, Jake!" someone yelled, "I'll take you on a four-to-one! Twenty on the pay if I win, and I'm with the boy. Five for you if he loses!"

"I'll do it!"

Red was taking care of the gate. He had Tobias's money and Joss's money. He had it all together because it would be given in one lump sum to the winner, when that was decided. He had made arrangements with the town banker to receive the money for Joss, if Joss won, so that he wouldn't have to be responsible for it on the long journey home.

Hank moved among the spectators, still glorying in his hawker's role of selling the show to the public.

Joss, with the collie beside him, was stationed on a bench near the gate. He was telling the dog to behave, not even to growl, when the wild sow came into the arena.

Tobias stood in front of the gate that barred the sow. The sow stood behind the chute, staring out through the bars, red-eyed and silent. When Red called time, Tobias would lift the gate and step up into the protected spectator area.

Sterling stuffed his hand back into his pocket. He didn't want people to see it shaking.

225

He wanted to call over to Joss and tell him that his mouth was dry, and would he please bring him a drink of water. But he didn't.

He wanted to stand up from the platform and run out of here, to run and run and run, clear back to his home in New York, where everything was quiet and peaceful, where no one mocked him or challenged him or expected him to do great things.

Try as he might to keep Uncle Morris close, between him and his fear, it did not work. That was why he was here, for Uncle Morris, but Uncle Morris kept skittering away, way back some place in his mind, and the terror came between. It was here now, fresh and awful, the terror of losing, the terror of ridicule, the terror of not being able to lift a hand without it shaking like a flopping fish.

Sterling raised his head. He could not breathe in the smother of his fear. He lifted his head and gazed out to the horizon, out to the west.

The sun was blinking out of sight, down over the low purple mountains in the distance.

Sterling wondered if Uncle Morris was watching it, too, back there in his bedroom on the ranch. —Uncle Morris, Uncle Morris, are you feeling pain? I hope that you aren't suffering—

"Time!" Red's voice clanged out over the auction yard. "Get ready there, son! Tobias, let's have that wild sow out here!"

Sterling stood up on the platform. He lifted the hand

that held the riata and bowed around to the people that encircled him like a gigantic nest. He didn't see the people, though, not clearly. Uncle Morris was in the way. He was lying there on his bed. He was saying, "I'll be ready to go back East when you get back."

And then the mad sow was spurting from the chute.

Sterling took a step backward and tossed a loop into the air.

The riata came to life. It was no longer a coil of lifeless, braided cowhide, but a thing alive and singing. It rose and fell and twirled and floated, a thin, black ring against the golden sunset.

The hog was nearing him, now, coming up on his right side, bounding toward him in lightning streaks.

Sterling's body swayed out to the right and twisted like the half turn of a screw. His free hand stood out from his body like a wing, balancing his stance. The loop, about the circumference of a barrel top, whirred counterclockwise, at the level of Sterling's shoulder. Its angle was slanted, as if spinning against an unseen roof.

Then, quicker than the eye could follow, the lasso came down.

The hog was head and shoulders beyond Sterling when the riata descended.

The streak of leather dipped under the sow's hooves, over its head, and off its rump.

The empty lasso dived, twisting, to the ground, as if, for a fraction of a second, it were angry and spitting. Then it flopped over, limp and dead.

Laughter welled up around Sterling. It was a kind of triumphant laughter that said, "I told you so! See there, it is impossible!" It reached Sterling like a rumble of distant thunder.

"Try again!" someone shouted, and the crowd took up the chant. "Try again! Try again!" The tone of the cry told Sterling something more. It told him: This is fun! Of course you can't rope a hog, but it is fun watching you try!

Sterling gulped air into his dying lungs and glanced over at Red, and then at Tobias, who was there at Red's side already, waiting for his money. Would they let him try again?

Red had a hand up, waving it, asking everyone to be quiet.

A hush fell quickly on the crowd.

"If the lad tries again or not," Red announced, "it will be this gentleman's say so!" He indicated Tobias.

Tobias shook his head. "I won fair and square!" his voice clapped angrily. "I want my winnings!"

Joss appeared at Red's side, holding Firetop on a leash. He unfastened his belt and took from the inside pockets coins and twenty-dollar gold pieces.

"Here's eighty dollars more, Tobias," he said, his voice cool and business-like. "Give Sterl one more chance. If he wins, I'll keep this and our bet money that Red's holding. If Sterl loses, it's all yours." He handed the money to Red.

"What do you say, Tobias?" Red asked. "Are you on?"

228

Tobias stared at the gold coins being passed to Red. He nodded. "He can't do it," he barked. "I seen him try once before. I'll take that eighty, too."

"The gentleman says the lad can try once more, folks!"

There was applause, but now spectator feeling had changed; it was partisan.

"By cracky!" a white-haired rancher shrieked, "I believe you can do it, lad! Go easy! Don't get rattled, now!"

"In any case, we're for you, feller!"

Sterling felt the difference in the crowd's attitude. It had changed from one of indifference to one of friendliness. And more than this, he felt. He felt the faith of Joss, which was now pinpointed on him, a faith so strong that it warmed him and lifted him from the bitter pit of his shame and failure.

"This time, Uncle Morris," he vowed under his breath. "It's going to be this time!"

The sow was still snorting back and forth across the arena, though it had slowed to a single-footed gait.

Sterling took his prior stance. He knew what he had done wrong before—he had failed to twist in quickly enough with his wrist after the hold had been attained. That wouldn't happen again.

He slung a twirling loop into the air and waited for the hog to run by.

When the hog came and was in position, Sterling swung in, quick and steady, his hand obeying reflexes of long training.

This was what Tex had called the scoop shot, dipping

under the legs.

The riata flicked, and the noose sprung tight.

The hog went down, thudding and squawking like a frightened goose.

In the seconds that it lay stunned upon the ground, Sterling was down from the platform, the riata coiling here and there around the hog with expert swiftness.

When, after a lapse of six seconds, the hog made as if to leap to its feet and streak away, it only bounced itself over in a thudding roll. Its feet were pinned securely to its under side.

At first there was no sound from the crowd, except a unified, astounded gasp.

Then slowly, as if gathering momentum, a cheer swelled into the air.

"He did it, by grab!"

"Can you beat that!"

"Good lad! That's the way!"

Sterling felt it all, the boot-stamping and the hand-clapping, the yells and words. He felt Joss and Red and Hank clapping him on the shoulders.

Sterling smiled and smiled. He smiled until he thought his face would surely split, and still he smiled.

He was smiling at Uncle Morris, and at the world.

He was also smiling at himself.

Chapter 20

End of a Dream

Joss stuffed a quill into an inkwell and wrote:

January 14, 1891
New York City

Dear Ropejon:

We will be coming home right away. I want to get back. I want to see you and Top and Hank. I know you are taking care of things first-rate. Do you like the shirts and things? Don't think they cost too much. We still got money, after Pop's operation and the tickets home and buying things to take home.

Uncle John said Sterl can come back with us, maybe to stay. He said he sure liked the way Sterl looked.

Did Tobias get over his sick spell?

231

If you can't read this, have Hank read it. Tell him they got good oyster feeds here, too.

I got to quit now and go scrub. I got ink spilled on me.

Your friend,

Joss Melborne

P.S. Forgot to tell you that Pop can walk. His legs are wobbly, but so what?